Some of the praise for (

"One of the best authors ir today." – *Huntress Reviews*

"Bolen's writing has a certain elegance that lends itself to the era and creates the perfect atmosphere for her enchanting romances." – *RT Book Reviews*

Christmas at Farley Manor
Winner, Best Historical Novella of 2011 in Romance Through the Ages contest.

A Lady By Chance
Cheryl Bolen has done it again with another sparkling Regency romance. . .Highly recommended – *Happily Ever After*

With His Lady's Assistance (Regent Mysteries, Book 1)
"A delightful Regency romance with a clever and personable heroine matched with a humble, but intelligent hero. The mystery is nicely done, the romance is enchanting and the secondary characters are enjoyable." – *RT Book Reviews*

Finalist for International Digital Award for Best Historical Novel of 2011.

A Duke Deceived
"*A Duke Deceived* is a gem. If you're a Georgette Heyer fan, if you enjoy the Regency period, if you like a genuinely sensuous love story, pick up this first novel by Cheryl Bolen." – *Happily Ever After*

The Bride Wore Blue
Cheryl Bolen returns to the Regency England she knows so well. . .If you love a steamy Regency with a fast pace, be sure to pick up *The Bride Wore Blue*. – *Happily Ever After*

My Lord Wicked
Winner, International Digital Award for Best Historical Novel of 2011.

With His Ring
"Cheryl Bolen does it again! There is laughter, and the interaction of the characters pulls you right into the book. I look forward to the next in this series." – *RT Book Reviews*

To Take This Lord (originally titled An Improper Proposal)
"Bolen does a wonderful job building simmering sexual tension between her opinionated, outspoken heroine and deliciously tortured, conflicted hero." – *Booklist of the American Library Association*

One Golden Ring
"*One Golden Ring*...has got to be the most PERFECT Regency Romance I've read this year." – *Huntress Reviews*

Holt Medallion winner for Best Historical, 2006

The Counterfeit Countess
"This story is full of romance and suspense. . . No one can resist a novel written by Cheryl Bolen. Her writing talents charm all readers. Highly recommended reading! 5 stars!" – *Huntress Reviews*

"Bolen pens a sparkling tale, and readers will adore her feisty heroine, the arrogant, honorable Warwick and a wonderful cast of supporting characters." – *RT Book Reviews*

Daphne du Maurier award finalist for Best Historical Mystery

Protecting Britannia
It's fun to watch the case unfold in this nonstop action adventure...Graham and Britannia's second chance at love adds dimension to the story. – 4 STARS *RT Book Reviews*

Also by Cheryl Bolen

Regency Romance

The Brides of Bath Series:
    The Bride Wore Blue
    With His Ring
    The Bride's Secret
    To Take This Lord
The Regent Mysteries Series:
    With His Lady's Assistance (Book 1)
    A Most Discreet Inquiry (Book 2)
The Earl's Bargain
My Lord Wicked
A Lady by Chance
His Lordship's Vow
A Duke Deceived
One Golden Ring
Counterfeit Countess

Novellas:
Lady Sophia's Rescue
Christmas Brides (3 Regency Novellas)

Romantic Suspense

Texas Heroines in Peril Series:
    Protecting Britannia
    Capitol Offense
    A Cry in the Night
    Murder at Veranda House
Falling for Frederick

American Historical Romance

*A Summer to Remember (*3 American Historical Romances)

World War II Romance

It Had to be You

Inspirational Regency Romance

Marriage of Inconvenience

Christmas Brides
(Three Regency Novellas)

The Christmas Wish

Home for Christmas

Christmas at Farley Manor

Award Winning Author
Cheryl Bolen

CONTENTS

The Christmas Wish

1

Home for Christmas

89

Christmas at Farley Manor

169

The Christmas Wish

Cheryl Bolen

Copyright © 2012 by Cheryl Bolen

The Christmas Wish is a work of fiction. Names, characters, places, and incidents are the products of the author's imagination or are used fictitiously. Any resemblance to actual events, locales, or persons, living or dead, is entirely coincidental.

All rights reserved.

No part of this publication may be reproduced, stored or transmitted in any form or by any means without the prior written permission of the author.

Chapter 1

It was really appallingly deplorable the way Miss Annabelle Pemberton perked up at the very mention of that scoundrel Lord de Vere. She was rather like one of Papa's pointers at the sniff of a hare. Whilst she had sat dutifully drafting a letter to Aunt Smithington-Fortenoy she heard Simms admit the far-too-handsome, philandering viscount, who was calling upon her father. Like a half-wit, she abandoned her letter, leapt to her feet, and rushed to the corridor in time to see Simms shake a puff of snow from Lord de Vere's beaver hat. Had she a tail, it would have wagged.

Miss Pemberton might not be able to control her lamentable interest in all things de Vere, but years of careful grooming by refined ladies of rank had schooled her to never display emotion. Very calmly, she paused on the upper landing and coolly observed the only man who had ever ruffled her serene countenance.

Could one ever tire of looking at the man? Her gaze began at his fashionably styled dark brown hair and moved to those near-black eyes set in a very fine face that was memorable for the well-defined cleft in his square chin. Men—being generally incapable of such distinctions—might not be able to perceive his handsomeness, but there was nary a man in England who could fail to envy Lord de Vere's tall, lean-muscled frame, narrow waist, and long, well-formed legs.

The supremely confident peer spread those well-formed legs, planting his booted feet on the marble floor, and casually looked up. "There you are, Belle." The tenderness of his smile gave her a bubbling sensation. *Odious man!*

Her brows lowered. "You're to call me Miss Pemberton," she admonished as she started to descend the broad marble stairway. Since he had succeeded at age eighteen a dozen years ago, she had not once referred to him by his first name as she had when they were younger, and since she had left the schoolroom seven years previously no one had addressed her by her first name. Except for Lord de Vere.

"What man calls his sister Miss Pemberton?"

She stiffened. "You are *not* my brother." As she drew closer to him, she realized Lord de Vere's usual impeccable clothing was wrinkled, and dark stubble shaded his face.

"I shall always regard you as my little sister." The way he peered down at her with smoldering black eyes belied his words. She cautioned herself not to read too much into his seductive demeanor. Expertise in the seduction of females was a skill that apparently did not depress easily—even with one he considered a sibling. *Odious man.*

"Really, de Vere, you are much too old to expect Papa to bail you out of another scrape." She ran her eye over his disheveled state, scrunching her nose with distaste. "You have not been to bed, have you?"

"You know me too well." His head hung. "I've come from Newmarket."

"Then you've suffered heavy losses?"

He answered her with a solemn nod. "I pride

myself on my knowledge of horseflesh." He shrugged and gave her a half smile. "But my cursed horse came up lame."

That de Vere was noted for his knowledge of horses she could not deny. When he was a lad, the de Vere stables were said to be the finest in the kingdom. Before his father lost the de Vere fortune at the gaming tables. "So you've come to beg a loan from my father?"

His eyes went cold. "Since the day he ceased to be my guardian, I have never asked your father for a farthing."

"Then I beg your forgiveness for my assumption." Her father's friends from Parliament—and even his chums going back to his days at Oxford—were often borrowing money from her wealthy parent. It was a natural assumption that de Vere had come today for the same reason.

"Since your father has been as a father to me, I owe him the explanation for my embarrassment. I shouldn't like him to learn it from another source."

Since her Papa had no sons of his own, he *had* rather regarded de Vere as a son—even if she had *not* regarded him as a brother.

Simms shuffled into the central hallway where they stood. "Mr. Pemberton will see you in his library, my lord."

Her worry over her father was somewhat relieved because he'd at least been able to leave his bed and move to the library.

De Vere spun back to her and sketched a bow.

Despite her resolve not to do so, she watched as he walked away, a full head taller than dear, white-headed Simms. The cocky, almost-arrogant demeanor that had defined de Vere during these years of hedonism suddenly vanished. She was reminded now of the thin lad he'd been with gangly legs and arms he'd yet to grow into and of his forlornness on becoming an orphan at eighteen. And something twisted in her heart.

She had far too many worries twisting her heart at present. When would the physician come? She had sent for him that morning. The fact that Papa had condescended to allow her to summon Marsden filled her with dread.

The prospect of facing his well-respected former guardian made de Vere feel rather like a lad who'd been summoned to the headmaster's. He smirked over the irony. De Vere had been an exemplary student with a hunger for learning. It was many years later that he became dissolute.

As he trod behind the stooped butler along Pemberton's opulent hallway of marble and gilt and hung with massive paintings by Italian masters, de Vere remembered what his father had told him about Robert Pemberton's former dissolute ways. For nine and forty years the enormously wealthy rake gave no indication he would ever settle into respectability. Yet for a woman who captured his heart and for the daughter who held that heart in her firm grasp, Robert Pemberton had abandoned his profligate ways as easily as a hound sheds its winter coat.

De Vere entered a library paneled in rich, dark wood and observed Pemberton sitting in front of the fire, a thick tome on his lap, spectacles dangling at the tip of his nose as he read. A perfect picture of respectability.

Unlike his former ward.

When Pemberton looked up at him, he smiled. "Come sit by me, my boy. The fire feels good to these old bones."

"These bones of mine can certainly welcome the warmth." De Vere pulled a chair in front of the fire and sat. "It's a beastly cold day."

Pemberton scrutinized him much as one would a portrait in the Royal Gallery. De Vere braced himself for a rebuke. Not that his kindly mentor had ever chastised him.

"I am concerned for you," Pemberton finally said. "I have known you for three decades and have never known you to step out of de Vere House unless your appearance was perfection."

"But you see, I did not step from my home this morning." He drew a long breath. "I've come from Newmarket."

The exceedingly long pause which followed was almost palpable. Finally, the elder man spoke. "I take it the races did not progress in an agreeable manner for you."

"To be perfectly honest, sir, they could not have been worse."

"'Tis a good thing your properties are tied up in the entail, then."

De Vere nodded. "Indeed. The pity of it is, I cannot afford to occupy either of my properties. That's why I've come to you today."

"I shall be happy to loan you money to tide you over."

"That is *not* why I've come." Anger surged through him. He had unwisely gambled and lost. Now he was prepared to face the consequences of his mistakes. "I came so you would be the first to learn that I plan to lease both the house on Cavendish Square and Hamptonworth. With vastly reduced living expenses and the income from the properties, I should be able to right my situation in a year or two. I, ah. . . didn't want you to learn of my indiscretions from someone else." Even worse, he hated to lose the man's admiration.

"I am a very wealthy man. You are the closest thing I'll ever have to a son. I wish to *give* you the money you lost."

De Vere stood and spoke icily. "There is nothing that could persuade me to accept it."

Mr. Pemberton shrugged. "Sit down, my boy. Just because you won't accept my assistance doesn't mean I must be deprived of a visit with you."

De Vere chuckled as he returned to his chair.

"'Tis a pity," the elder man continued, "but I know you won't change your mind about accepting my help. In this, you're entirely too much like your stubborn father."

"You, more than anyone, understood the complex man who was my father." The two had gone through Eton and Oxford together and had been the closest of friends until the day his father died.

His gaze raked over the man beside him. He had never noticed when Pemberton's hair had gone white. Were his father still alive, he would likely resemble this aged man who sat next to him. He wondered if the eighth decade of life would have tamed his roguish father, wondered if he himself would ever be tamed.

"Because we were too damned much alike!"

"With one exception, sir. You abandoned hedonism once you wed."

The elder man nodded. "I believe you, too, will

when a pretty thing sweeps you off your feet." He sat up straighter in his chair. "Which brings up another subject that concerns you."

"You think I should marry."

"Indeed. You need to marry an heiress."

"I agree, but I am incapable of offering my title to the highest bidder, so to speak."

"I understand. You're holding out for a romantic marriage."

"If a man must be forced to spend his life joined to one woman, it should be with a woman he *wants* to spend the rest of his life with."

"I've lived a long time and learned a thing or two along the way. It has been my observation that, in many cases, once a man and woman are wed—even when there was no love involved—and have children together a deep bond of friendship forms between them, and often that friendship turns to love."

"And in just as many cases, the shackles make the couple miserable. Look at the Duke of Wellington!"

"I will own, his marriage is wretched. He can barely stand to be in the same room with his wife."

"I'd rather go my grave a bachelor."

"I pray that you don't. It would make me very unhappy to think that no descendent of you or your father would ever occupy Hamptonworth. It would be very sad to leave this earth and know that no part of you remains."

"Oblige me by speaking no more of such morbid thoughts."

Pemberton smiled. "You must tell me about your misfortunes at Newmarket."

"Misfortune does not begin to sum up my sad

experience. You will remember me speaking of that fleet chestnut . . ."

Long after Lord de Vere took his leave of Pemberton House—without seeking to say goodbye to her—the physician came. She practically flew down the stairs to speak with him before he went to see her father.

The courtly physician, who was favored by at least two of the royal princesses, bowed as he took Miss Pemberton's hand and kissed the air above her glove. "You are most fortunate not to have to leave your home on a day like today, Miss Pemberton. 'Tis beastly cold out there."

"I have made sure Papa does not leave and have encouraged him to sit near the fire where it's warmer."

Marsden nodded. "Very good. Your father is getting on in years. How old is he now?"

"Three and seventy. Because his father lived to be ninety, I've always assumed Papa would, too, but this past week I've become most alarmed."

"What seems to be wrong with him?"

She drew a deep breath, hating to say the words, hating to think of what this ailment could signify. "Discomfort in his chest."

Mr. Marsden's brows squeezed into a vee. "That is not good, not good at all in a man of that age." The physician who had not yet reached fifty flicked his gaze to the stairway. "I shall have to examine him."

"Yes, of course. Will you come to me after you've seen him?"

"Most certainly, my dear."

She went to sit before the fire in the drawing room. One of the footmen had placed a tall arm chair that was upholstered in green velvet a few feet from the hearth. Settling her lap desk on her thighs, she completed the letter to Aunt Smithington-Fortenoy, folded it, then sat there peering at the window. A thin sheen of frost pooled at the bottom of each pane, and thick gray fog obliterated even the view of Lord Conningham's tall, narrow house just across the street. It *was* a dreadful day to be out of doors.

Would they even be able to travel to Upper Barrington for Christmas? She had given the matter considerable thought. With rugs and hot bricks and mufflers swathing his frail neck, Papa should tolerate the ride well enough. Surrey was not so terribly far from London, after all.

Yet their country house on two thousand acres of rolling parkland and pastures seemed as far removed from London as Istanbul. Many happy Christmases had been spent there with those she loved, gathering holly and skating on the frozen lake and lighting the Yule log and worshiping at tiny St. Stephen's on the morning of Christ's birth.

She wouldn't like it at all if a snowstorm prevented them from going to Upper Barrington.

After the passage of a quarter of an hour, the door to the drawing room came open, and Mr. Marsden stood there, framed by the massive, pedimented doorway, an achingly solemn look on his ruddy face.

Her breathing accelerated violently. Her palms sweat. Her throat went dry. She was incapable of giving voice to that which she dreaded most. She merely stared at the physician, noticing absurdly unimportant things like the bulbous nose indicative of a man who overindulged in strong spirits and the sterling buttons on his gray wool jacket.

She came to realize Mr. Marsden wanted to tell her the grievous pronouncement no more than she wanted to hear it. Eventually he cleared his throat. She fought the urge to cover her ears as she'd done as a girl when she did not want to hear unwelcome words. She was no longer that child. Now she was a woman of three and twenty. She rose, held her head high, and faced the physician, a querying expression on her face.

"I must prepare you, Miss Pemberton. This is likely the last Christmas you will ever spend with your father."

A burst of hot tears gushed to her eyes. She made no effort to wipe away the rivulets that began to drip from her cheekbones and chin. "You have told my father?"

He nodded solemnly.

"Then I must go to him." A sob broke as she turned toward the door.

Before she could face her dear Papa, though, she must attempt to cheer him. For the past two weeks, his sole source of pleasure had come from sampling the pickles sent from his cousin, Betsy Blaine-Ramsbury, who zealously guarded the recipe that had been used in Papa's grandmother's home and, according to Papa, produced the only crave-worthy pickles on the planet.

She descended the stairs to the basement and raced to the kitchen where she fetched one, long, delicious pickle. Cook noticed her reddened eyes and glistening cheeks but was too polite to comment upon it. She wiped her hands on her apron, took the pickle, and placed it on a delicate ivory and gilt saucer. "Yer papa will want more than one."

"If my papa was permitted to have his way, all of Cousin Betsy's pickles would already be gone."

Cook smiled. "Indeed they would."

By the time Miss Pemberton had mounted three flights of stairs to her father's library, her tears had dried.

She tapped upon his door.

"I know it's you, Belle, and I'll not allow you in if you're crying."

A smile tweaked at the corners of her mouth. "I'm not crying."

"Then you may enter."

Her white-haired father sat before the fire, a blanket spread across his lap, his discarded book fanned open on the Turkey carpet beneath his chair. He had never looked so frail.

"I've brought you one of Cousin Betsy's pickles."

He smiled at her. "I knew I could count on you to brighten my day, my dearest." Neither the sparkling blue of his eyes nor the stridency of his voice bespoke a man in his decline.

He greedily bit into the pickle. "You've spoken with Marsden?"

She nodded solemnly as she lowered herself into the chair next to him. She supposed it was the chair Lord de Vere had sat upon.

"I suppose he told you this will be my last Christmas?"

"You mustn't believe everything the fellow says. After all, he's a man, and man is not infallible."

"You, my dearest, must not always be so optimistic. I am an old man. I've lived a long, exceedingly happy life. For nine and forty years I indulged my every whim. Then I was blessed to fall in love with the best of women, whose last act on this earth was to give me the child who would be the joy of my life and the comfort of my old age. Save but one thing, I could die perfectly happy right now."

She knew very well what that *one thing* was. "You mustn't worry about leaving me alone. It's by my own choice that I'm not wed."

He availed himself of the last bite of pickle and savored it for several seconds of appreciative *um-um-umming* before speaking. "I've worried that you refused to marry because you did not want to leave me alone."

She shook her head. "First, my dear parent, you must realize that any man who was ever foolish enough to attempt to court me did so in order to secure my fortune. I know it's difficult for you to realize, but I am not considered a beauty."

"But you *are* pretty!"

"I am short and plain and far too particular in my tastes to settle for any man desperate enough to pay me homage."

"We have had this discussion before, and we shall never see eye to eye on it."

"Then I must change the topic of discussion. Pray, Papa, will you feel up to the journey to Upper Barrington?"

"Of course I will! I've spent every Christmas for the past thirty years there, and it's my next-to-fondest desire to spend my last one there."

She must humor him. Bless her dearest father, he was taking the news of his demise remarkably well. "It does seem that since this *may* be. . ." She had to pause, to fortify herself in order to utter that which was so very painful to acknowledge. ".

. . your last Christmas, I should seek to grant you one last wish. What *is* it that is your *next-to* fondest desire?" She knew very well what his answer would be.

"I cannot die content unless I know you will be taken care of by a husband who loves and cherishes you."

She gave a bitter laugh. "'Twould be easier to find forests in the desert."

He shook his head adamantly. "I strongly disagree with you."

"I daresay you're just worried I'll turn out to be a peculiar spinster of dubious repute like Lady Hester Stanhope."

Her father rolled his eyes. "If I believed that, I'd shoot myself right now."

She giggled. She could not believe she was sitting there giggling just minutes after the physician had informed her Papa was dying. "Pray, Papa, have you ever encountered a man whom you think would suit me?"

He nodded sheepishly. How could a man with such spark in his eyes be nearing death?

"Oblige me, then," she said, folding her arms across her chest, "by revealing to me who this man is."

"He was at our home this very afternoon."

Her eyes rounded. "I believe Mr. Marsden is already married."

"I wasn't referring to Marsden," he snapped.

Her pulse began to pound. Not once in her three and twenty years had her father ever tried to play matchmaker between his well-loved daughter and his well-admired ward. Had he always held the opinion that she and de Vere would suit?

It was true he had never maligned de Vere no matter how debauched the viscount was. She was shocked her protective father would even consider marrying her to so dissolute a man.

Of course, de Vere *did* have his good qualities. He was vastly intelligent. He *had* always been excessively kind to her, even when she was but six years old and he a lad of thirteen—which, she had to admit, many lads of that age would not have been. He also took his duties in Parliament seriously and was respected by his peers.

Her heart fluttered. And, of course, his stunning good looks could not be forgotten. Not that anyone born with a womb could.

The movement of her father's hand caught her eye. He clutched at his chest, his brow furrowed.

She leaped from her chair. "Papa! Papa! Are you all right?"

A pained expression on his face, he nodded. "It's that same dashed pain."

At least he could speak. She sank back into her chair. And suddenly she realized she just might be able to grant her father his last Christmas wish.

Chapter 2

Her hands stuffed into an ermine muff, a thick Kashmir muffler wrapping her neck like plump layers of tobacco leaf about a cigar, and a heavy rug secured over her lower extremities, Miss Pemberton settled back in the family's luxurious carriage. Whether the distressingly queer feelings in the pit of her stomach could be attributed to Papa's dire prognosis or to her impending meeting with Lord de Vere—if he should be at home—she did not know. Throughout the short carriage ride to Cavendish Square, her heart beat unaccountably rapidly.

When the coachman came to a stop in front of de Vere House, she grew even more nervous. The burst of cold air when he opened the carriage door nearly persuaded her to slam it shut and stay within the secure confines of the coach.

But then she thought of Papa's wish.

Her own feelings seemed rather insignificant. Therefore, she held her head high, stepped down to the pavement, and strode to his lordship's front door. Because the coachman had already announced her, the butler swung open the door before she could knock. "I have sent word to Lord de Vere that Miss Pemberton is calling. Allow me to show you to the drawing room."

She followed the fairly youthful fellow up a flight of stairs in the airy stairwell which was lighted from a glass-domed roof. The drawing room was much smaller than the one at her house but was furnished in the same neoclassical lines adopted by Robert Adam—whom Papa had engaged to do the London interiors before she was born.

"I beg your forgiveness," the butler said. Each word he spoke was accompanied by chilled puffs of vapor. "For not having a fire lit here. It is just that his lordship seldom receives callers."

A char woman noiselessly entered the room and began to light the fire.

Miss Pemberton had heard her housekeeper remark on the high cost of coal. Was Lord de Vere so strapped for funds that he slept in freezing cold rooms?

Wickedly, she hoped that it was so. Then he might be more agreeable to her bizarre proposal. She turned to face the butler. "I believe I prefer to keep my pelisse and muff." Her pelisse of coral colored velvet, trimmed with ermine kept her adequately warmed.

Whilst the woman was building the fire, Miss Pemberton strolled to the street-facing window. It was tall and narrow in the Italianate style and was draped in faded green silk so brittle that she feared it would fall away like an ash if she touched it.

She had expected to be able to look over the square, but she saw nothing save the fog as heavy as curtain obliterating any view.

"Belle."

She had not heard him enter the chamber. Her heartbeat roared as she turned to face him. Her solemn gaze stroked him. "You've shaved."

He nodded. "Please, come sit on the settee. We shall have a fire warming things in a few minutes."

The gilt settee she sat on was covered in striped gold and green silk that did not appear to be faded. She supposed it had rarely been sat upon. De Vere had lived here as a bachelor for the past dozen years. She supposed even the draperies to this chamber had seldom been opened during that time.

De Vere sat next to her, a concerned look on his exceedingly handsome face. "You haven't been here since you were a girl."

She smiled up at him. "Not since I was twelve. Nothing has changed."

"Except me," he said with a frown.

"You sound as if you don't approve of what you've become."

"Can you blame me?"

As she looked into those dark, soulful eyes, something melted inside her. Even her trembling subsided. All she could think of was the frightened, sad boy he'd been the day of his father's funeral. Gaining a title at so tender an age was bound to affect a lad on the precipice of manhood. And *not* for the better.

A shrug was her only answer.

"Pray, Belle, to what do I owe the pleasure?"

"I'm afraid I've not come on a pleasurable mission."

He lurched toward her. "Has something happened to your father?"

In that fraction of a second she understood that this man who sat next to her cared very deeply for her father. No one could feign such a look of distress or alter a voice to convey such genuine fear.

She nodded. Which had the effect of releasing

the floodgates. Great, whimpering sobs broke forth from her.

"Has he died?"

She shook her head, a torrent of tears streaming down her face, her shoulders hitching on each fresh sob.

He drew her into his embrace, tracing circles upon her back, stroking her hair, and murmuring comforting words. "It's all right, love. We can face this. You must tell me everything." He offered her his own very large handkerchief.

She blotted her tears and attempted to blow her nose in a dainty manner while gathering her composure. "You must forgive my outburst," she finally said.

"There's nothing to forgive. I'd like to think I am the one you would turn to in your time of distress. I want you to think of me as your elder brother."

That comment sent her wailing anew. How could one propose marriage to a man who thought of her as a sister?

He hauled her into his embrace. "Belle, Belle. You must tell me what's wrong."

Once more she took his handkerchief and wiped away the evidence of her crying, drew a long breath, then looked up into his stupendously handsome face. It was a face she could never tire of. What would it be like to be married to him, to be able to gaze upon his physical perfection the first thing every morning and the last thing every night for the rest of her life?

"I had Marsden to look at Papa today. He's been complaining of discomfort in his. . . chest."

De Vere's brows lowered.

Her eyes watered again. This was very difficult,

but she was determined to speak of it without bawling. "Marsden said this will be Papa's last Christmas."

He winced and buried his head in his hands.

She was completely unprepared for such a blatant specimen of masculinity to take the dreadful news in such a way.

Now their roles were reversed, and she needed to stay composed until he recovered. A few minutes later he looked up and addressed her. "I must ease your father's mind. I must assure him that I will look after you."

She felt as if a huge chestnut was lodged in her throat. "That is precisely why I've come to you today."

He gave her a quizzing look. "Enlighten me, please."

"Papa says save for one thing, he could die perfectly happy today."

"And that one thing?"

"He wishes to see me wed."

"I don't see how I can hel- - - Oh, dear God, you can't mean. . .?"

She nodded ruefully. "My poor, delusional father thinks you and I would suit."

He sighed. "I couldn't possibly consider such a ridiculous thing! Why, it would be like marrying my own sister!"

"I assure you, Lord de Vere, I have never thought of you as a brother."

"Surely you can't put any credence to this silly notion of your father's?"

"Of course I don't think you and I would suit! You would be one of the last men in the kingdom whom I would ever consider for a husband. I shouldn't at all like being wed to profligate who keeps mistresses."

His eyes narrowed. "You're not to know of such things. And, besides, I no longer have any woman under my protection."

She put her hands to her waist. "And I shouldn't at all wish to wed a man who would take the fortune my grandfather built and wager it away at Newcastle and White's."

"You assume I would beg to marry you—which, *Miss Pemberton*, I have no intention of doing!"

His words were like a slap in the face. She had been prepared for him to reject her proposal, but she was unprepared for the vehemence of his objection. Tears stung her eyes once more. "I assure you, I have no intention of marrying a debauched man such as you."

She pounced to her feet, and the muff that had been in her lap fell to the Aubusson carpet. Lord de Vere stooped to pick it up. As he offered it to her, he asked, "Then why have you come?"

"Because I was prepared to sacrifice myself in order to grant my father his last Christmas wish."

His eyes flared with anger. "You, *Miss* Pemberton, are singular in the opinion that marrying me would be a sacrifice."

"Why, of all the arrogant men I have ever known, I do believe you go to the head of the queue." She shoved her hands in the muff, flipped the Kashmir muffler about her neck, and stormed to the door. "I cannot understand how my father could be so blinded to your multitude of faults!"

How could he let that sanctimonious spinster get him so riled? It was only by the greatest restraint he prevented himself from trailing in her stormy wake like some dumbstruck lad begging his governess's forgiveness. He had done nothing for which he needed to apologize! It was she who had impugned his character, she who asserted her abhorrence of marriage to him.

Shaking with anger, he went to his library, slammed the heavy door behind him, and poured himself a tall glass of brandy. Damn, but this room was cold! He rang for Majors.

Anticipating his master's needs, the butler eased open the door. "I perceive your lordship would like a fire built in the library."

"Why in the devil is this house so blasted cold?"

"Because your lordship suggested that to reduce the expense for coal we eliminate fires in the public rooms, since you never receive callers. Except for today."

"I'm sure it seemed like a very good idea at the time, but since I shall not brave the elements on this beastly day, I will require warmth in this chamber."

Before he completed his sentence, the char woman came waddling into the library and set about starting the fire.

"It appears, Majors, you've anticipated my request before I made it."

Majors bowed his head. "Will there be anything else, my lord?"

De Vere's eye skipped to the empty decanter on the silver tray. "Yes. Fetch me another bottle of brandy!"

Once the fire was going strong, de Vere began to pace the chamber, mumbling angrily to himself over the annoying Pemberton chit. After the passage of an hour and the consumption of three glasses of brandy, his anger toward his guardian's daughter subsided.

But it was replaced by something much worse.

Raw sorrow as painful as acid began to eat at him. Even though he was a mature man of thirty, he felt the need to turn to his former guardian in both good times and bad. The constancy of Robert Pemberton had given a certain solidity to his otherwise vagrant ways. Deep down, he'd always known that were he truly in need—whether that need be for a sympathetic ear or a timely financial rescue—he could always count on Mr. Pemberton. In many ways he'd been closer to him than he'd been to his own erratic, devil-may-care father.

He was reminded of Pemberton's words that very afternoon when he'd said de Vere had more in common with him than he had with his father. It was true. Except that by his fiftieth year, Pemberton replaced his wild ways with the affection and fidelity of a good father—something his own father had never managed.

Deep down, de Vere had always hoped to turn out in the same way as his guardian. For Robert Pemberton had become a man who was widely admired.

Most of all by William Addison, Viscount de Vere.

How painful it was to think that by the next Christmas, Robert Pemberton would be cold in his grave. De Vere finished the last swig in his glass. How horribly he would miss the man, how lonely his own world would become.

When night fell, de Vere wobbled up the stairs and collapsed upon his tall tester bed, sending Smith away without even allowing him to remove his boots. He wished to lose himself in the oblivion of a deep sleep, but he was not able to do so.

For his thoughts had once again turned to Annabelle Pemberton and why she had sought him out that day.

He felt honor bound to do his duty to the man who had always been there for him. Pemberton doted on Belle. De Vere understood her father would not want to leave her unprotected, uncared for.

He really ought to promise. . . No, he could *not* marry her! He didn't love her. At least not like a man loved a woman.

Why was he even thinking of this? Hadn't she made it perfectly clear that marriage to him repulsed her? Then why in the blazes had she come that day? Why had she brought up the topic of a marriage between them?

Because it was her father's last wish. His last Christmas wish.

And because they both loved Robert Pemberton, he knew he must grant the wish.

Chapter 3

How could she have said such wretched things to Lord de Vere? It wasn't as if he had ever treated her in any way that could possibly provoke such rebuke. Not once in her entire life had he ever been anything but exceedingly kind to her. Exactly as he was to his four sisters, three of whom were happily wed.

She frowned to herself. She did not like to admit it, but it was his very brotherliness that ignited her uncharacteristic fury. Truth be told, she had always wanted Lord de Vere to see her as a desirable female. Her thoughts flitted to the Beauties of the Ton with whom he had been linked over the years. In every physical comparison to those beauties, she came up wanting. To think a handsome viscount such as he could ever find her appealing (she couldn't aspire to attractive) was to demonstrate that she'd taken complete leave of her senses.

In her entire three and twenty years Miss Annabelle Pemberton had never displayed as regrettable conduct as she had at Lord de Vere's the previous day. She had scarcely slept all night as she mentally drafted a hundred notes of apology to him, not that any note could exonerate her from such an unwarranted attack upon his character. For the rude manner in which she had criticized him, she ought to fall on her knees and beg his forgiveness.

For it was nothing to her if Lord de Vere chose to ruin his life in gaming hells and courtesan's beds. His debauched ways hurt no one save himself.

Upon rising the next morning, the first thing she did was to jot down a single line to beg the viscount's forgiveness. She sealed it, called for her maid, and instructed her to see that it was delivered to de Vere.

Not five minutes had passed when Simms brought her a letter. She immediately saw that it came from de Vere, but she knew he could not possibly have received her apology that quickly.

With lowered brows, she broke his distinctive stag seal—the same his father had used.

My Dear Belle,
I beg that you do me the goodness of allowing me to call upon you at two this afternoon. In private.
de Vere

Dear God! Could this possibly mean what she thought it did? The very fact that he'd not addressed the note to Miss Pemberton—the name he'd called her in anger the previous day—indicated a softening toward her. Which she did not deserve.

She began to tremble. *He's going to ask me to marry him!*

Were he any other man, she would have been vastly suspicious of monetary motives. But a man—a titled man—of such extraordinary good looks could easily take his pick of any heiress in all of the three kingdoms. Besides, de Vere was far too proud to accept even sixpence from her generous father, no matter how desperate his need.

He was preparing to offer himself as the last gift to a man beloved by them both.

And she had never been more ashamed of herself.

She immediately rang for Sally, and when that devoted servant came, Miss Pemberton said, "I wish to charge you with a nearly impossible task."

The maid cocked her fair head. "What would that be, miss?"

"You are to render me pretty. Do something exotic with my hair and help me select my most flattering gown."

They had three hours in which to prepare her, and in that time Miss Pemberton slipped into and subsequently discarded some fifteen gowns before she found one that satisfied her. When two o'clock came, she knew she had done all that was possible to appear worthy of a proposal of marriage from the most handsome aristocrat in the *ton*.

Somehow, he'd never thought he would marry before he reached nine and forty. Without ever giving it much thought, he supposed he'd always wished to emulate the man he admired so thoroughly. But never—not even in his most inebriated state—had he ever thought he could marry a woman he didn't love.

As he sat there in the Pemberton drawing room awaiting the young woman whose hand in marriage he was going to seek, he realized he did love Belle—but not like he had hoped to love a wife. Despite that she was a sharp-tongued, self-assured only child of a doting, elderly father who just happened to be in possession of one of the heftiest purses in all of England, Miss Annabelle Pemberton had always elicited in him a strong sense of protectiveness. One could not wish to protect a female one did not care about. He loved Belle as he loved Libby, Charlotte, Anne, and Georgiana—his sisters.

He thought of Pemberton's words the day before when he spoke of a husband and wife growing to love one another. After they had children together.

Bedding Belle, begetting a child with Belle? Even the pondering of such a thing was shocking, but the fact such a plan met with Mr. Pemberton's favor sanctioned it.

De Vere respected no man as much as he respected Robert Pemberton.

The door to the drawing room opened, and Belle glided into the room. He found himself observing her as if for the first time. Now he attempted to regard her as a prospective suitor. Which was deuced difficult! Look at her! She was as short as an eleven-year-old girl. His gaze whisked over her from the top of her flaxen locks, which were swept back from her face like that of a Grecian goddess, and along the gentle curve of her pale blue gown that swelled at her breasts.

What the devil? When had Miss Pemberton grown such womanly looking breasts? Because he was knowledgeable about women's undergarments, he knew how stays smashed a woman's bosom until the tops of the breasts spilled out of the tight laces. Is that what Miss Pemberton had done today? He could not remember ever before being aware of Miss Pemberton's . . . ah, breasts.

How old was she now? He distinctly

remembered she was seven years younger than he, which would make her three and twenty. She obviously had not just sprouted a bosom. How could he have failed to notice such . . . protuberances before? Because he was not in the habit of lusting after his guardian's well-protected, much-beloved only child.

He stood, favored her with a smile, and bowed. "Your beauty robs me of words." Surprisingly, he spoke the truth.

He had never previously thought of Miss Pemberton as a beauty, but on this day she was truly pretty.

Her face, while not gawk-worthy, was free of flaws. And her pale blue eyes were very fine.

She opened her mouth as if to protest, then must have thought better of it. Was she so unaccustomed to receiving praise? "Thank you, my lord. Please have a seat. Should you wish to be closer to the fire? It's another wretchedly chilly day." She eyed him, smiling. "It was very good of you to bestir yourself."

Was this the same chit who'd castigated him the previous day? She was being much more agreeable than normal. She even waited to see where he sat before she took her own seat beside him. They ended up on a silken settee closest to the hearth.

"I thank you for sending me the very kind note," he began.

"A note can in no way express my remorse, my lord. I had no right to speak to you in such a manner. I don't know what came over me. I could not sleep last night because I so desperately wished I could retract the awful things I said." She swallowed and peered up at him. "Because of my cruel words, it may be difficult for you to believe that I *am* excessively fond of you."

"As I am of you, Miss Pemberton." What in the blazes had gotten into him? He hadn't meant to lie to her and claim an attachment that wasn't there. Not that being fond of someone translated to being in love with them. He would never tell a woman—especially Belle—he was in love with her unless he meant it.

"Then can you forgive me?"

He took her hand. He hadn't meant to touch her. "I have forgotten it already."

He continued to hold her small hand within his. She had likely never before been in so intimate a setting with a man.

"Why the change in your address to me, my lord?"

It took him a minute to realize what she was referring to. Since she had walked through that door today, he had not once called her by the name he had used for three and twenty years. Was it because he was suddenly seeing her as something other than Mr. Pemberton's little girl, something different than a sister? He drew a deep breath. "I suppose it's because I'm doing my dashed best *not* to think of you as a sister."

It took several seconds—seconds as silent as a graveyard—before he could look her in the eye. Neither of them was foolish enough not to know why he had come that afternoon.

Their eyes met and held. Because his strong, long-fingered hand continued to clasp hers, the connection between them was profound. At least it was to her. It was certainly the most intimate gesture she had ever shared with a member of the opposite sex. (A pity the mere holding of a hand would seem rather insipid to a well-known rake like he.)

Her heartbeat began to pulse. "Oh," she finally managed. He was going to ask for her hand in marriage. She felt unbelievably feminine. And small. And, most of all, remorseful.

This was not how it was supposed to be! In her dreams, Lord de Vere begged for her hand in marriage while professing his deep love. Even if he asked for her hand today, she knew he would not lie and say he was in love with her.

But *her* feelings did not signify now. A union between her and Lord de Vere would bring joy to her father. It was, after all, his last Christmas wish.

Lord de Vere cleared his throat. "Because you are your father's daughter and are blessed with his intelligence, you realize why I've come today?"

She answered with a nod.

"Then I must ask if you're prepared to sacrifice yourself in order to grant your father his last Christmas wish."

To her complete mortification, she began to wail. Again. Lord de Vere was merely speaking his mind. Marrying her would be a mammoth sacrifice on his part—which was not even remotely like the romantic declaration she had always hoped for.

For the second time in as many days, she flattened the side of her face into his manly chest while he—rather too much like an elder brother—attempted to comfort her whilst handing her another handkerchief.

"What's the matter, love? You know this union will cheer your father."

"I am," sniff, sniff, "not crying because of my father."

He stiffened. "Then you object to me?"

"That is not why I am crying, either." She attempted to wipe away her tears with his handkerchief.

There went those blasted circles he was tracing upon her back! Did he have any idea how seductive such a gesture was?

"Then I am relieved."

"I am not." She straightened and glared at him, even knowing she must look wretched with her reddened eyes.

His brows lowered. "What have I done to offend you, Belle?"

At least he had reverted to calling her Belle. Even if it was being "brotherly" on his part, it sounded much more intimate, much more in keeping with the mood evoked with the hand-holding business. (Which, she had to admit, she rather liked.) "I daresay there's not another lady in the kingdom who is being told marriage to her is a sacrifice."

"I didn't say marrying you would be a sacrifice! I said your marriage to me would be a sacrifice."

"It's what you were thinking. Admit it. Marrying me would be a sacrifice—a sacrifice you'd be willing to offer on the shrine to my father."

He remained silent. "I will *not* say that. Allow me to ask you one thing."

Her eyes rounded. "What?"

"Why do you hold me in animosity?"

As she sat there studying his pensive face from the black eyes to the notch in his chin, something softened inside her. De Vere was without a doubt the most noble man she had ever encountered. Yet despite the "sacrifice" he was prepared to make, she had treated him shabbily. And despite his abundance of attributes, her cruel words had wounded him.

She was obliged to assure him of her admiration. "I could never hold you in animosity. Forgive me if I gave that impression. If I didn't have strong feelings of affection toward you, I wouldn't be sitting here right now."

"Then, my dear Miss Pemberton," he began, now tracing circles on the palm of her hand, his dark eyes never leaving hers, "I beg that you do me the goodness of consenting to become my wife."

Even though this man requesting her hand in marriage, this man who destroyed her complacency with those incessant circles pressed into her hand, was the only man she had ever aspired to wed, this wasn't the way she had always pictured it. Her eyes misted, but she was determined not to cry. "It is very kind of you to offer yourself, my lord. While there may be some who will believe you're marrying me for my fortune, I know that is not your motive. Are you prepared for the wicked things which may be said of you for marrying a plain heiress?"

"First of all, you are not plain! If you think that, you have not peered into your looking glass today. Secondly, you have not actually accepted my proposal."

Her gaze never leaving his, she nodded solemnly. "Despite the wretched things I said to you yesterday, there is not another man in the kingdom whom I would prefer over you." At least she hadn't blathered on about being in love with him. A lady had her pride.

"Would that I were worthy of your flattery."

She was disappointed he hadn't countered with a similar compliment. "You do have many fine traits, and I do accept your proposal of marriage."

He brought her hand to his lips and kissed it. "Your father believes marriage would be a steadying influence upon me, one which would restore respectability to the de Vere name."

"I agree with my father."

"There is one problem I see with this . . . this sham marriage."

"It's not to be a sham marriage, my lord. Only a real marriage would please my father."

"Oh, I intend to marry you in a legally binding ceremony."

"Then what is this problem you foresee?"

"No matter how fond your father is of me, he will require that you marry a man who will love and cherish you."

Yes, her father would. "A rather difficult requirement."

He gave her a kindly smile. "Not entirely. I have always held you in great fondness, the same brotherly affection I have for my sisters."

She drew in a deep breath. "As much as I want this marriage—in order to grant my father's last Christmas wish—I cannot consent to it without extracting one promise from you."

"What is that?"

"You must give me your solemn promise that you will *not* think of me as a sister!"

He looked perplexed. "How can I govern thoughts I've held for two decades?"

She put hands to hips. "May I suggest you force yourself to think of my breasts!"

His gaze flicked to those plump objects on her chest, then quickly returned to her face. She was serious.

And she was likely right. If he forced himself to think of Miss Pemberton's breasts, he was much less likely to think of her as a sister. "I shall do my best to comply with your wishes, Miss Pemberton."

"And now that I am to be your wife," she said with some authority, "I shall not object if you call me Belle."

Your wife. It seemed almost unfathomable to him that he was having this discussion, that he was on the precipice of marriage. If someone had told him a week ago that he was going to marry Annabelle Pemberton, he would have told that person he had attics to let. Yet here he was, making preparations to wed Belle. He nodded. "Soon you shall be Lady de Vere."

"How soon?"

"I can procure a special license today, and we can marry tomorrow."

A slow smile spread across her face. "I believe that will make a splendid Christmas gift for Papa."

If he had not agreed with that, he wouldn't be standing there. He nodded. "I shall now go to your father."

He had sat in that good man's library more than he had ever sat with his own father in their library. Most of those times, he'd found the Pemberton library a comforting place.

But that was not the case today.

Today he felt almost an intruder as he strolled into the dark chamber. A fire blazed in the hearth, and the red velvet draperies were open to reveal dark skies on this bitterly cold day. During previous visits to this room of handsome floor-to-ceiling books and walnut paneling, he thought of Robert Pemberton as his indulgent guardian and later as his former guardian, but today he thought of him as a protective father to a much-beloved only child.

Mr. Pemberton sat reading in front of the fire. It pained de Vere to realize Pemberton was an old man. "Ah, de Vere! Do have a seat."

Somehow, de Vere did not think it proper to sit back and ask for Miss Annabelle Pemberton's hand as casually as commenting upon the weather. "If you do not object, sir, I prefer to stand."

"Can't say that I blame you. Despite that this is the warmest room in the house, it is much more comfortable standing in front of the fire. Mind if I join you?"

"If you feel up to it- - -"

Pemberton smiled as he rose, took the poker, and began to probe at the fire. "I see my daughter's been telling you about that rubbish from Marsden."

"Mr. Marsden is a well-respected physician."

"So my daughter says."

"Of course even the wisest physicians are not always correct."

"That is true."

"It's just that if the man's prognosis *should* prove accurate, I wish to assure you that Miss Pemberton will be well taken care of."

"Miss Pemberton? When, my boy, have you ever referred to my daughter by that formal name?"

De Vere relaxed and favored his mentor with a smile. "Since I started to think of her as a suitor would. In fact, sir, I've come to beg for her hand in marriage."

Pemberton stopped poking at the fire and turned to him, a stupendous smile breaking across his face. How could a man who seemed so alive be dying?

The very thought of losing Robert Pemberton was painful.

"I surmise my daughter has informed you that I would approve of the match?"

"Indeed, sir."

The older man nodded. "Good. It is very good of you, very good of you, indeed. You have my complete blessing. When will this . . . occurrence take place?"

De Vere swallowed. "Is tomorrow too soon?"

"Tomorrow will be very good. I'll have my man of business draw up the contracts at once, and you can sign them in the morning." He offered a handshake to his prospective son-in-law.

As their hands came firmly together, de Vere was nearly overcome with powerful emotions. It was as if this handshake symbolized the joining of their two houses.

Forever.

Chapter 4

She wept at her wedding. For most of the ceremony—held in the drawing room at Pemberton House with only her father and de Vere's one sister who was still in London attending—she attempted to exude a graceful serenity she was far from feeling. All of her life she had managed quite nicely to avoid any public display of emotions.

Only when she was with de Vere did her composure vanish like yesterday's snow. Whether it be chastising his gambling or collapsing into tears, her tight control had a decidedly awkward tendency to unravel when she was in the viscount's presence.

Lord de Vere's behavior this day was excessively amiable. As she strode up to him whilst he stood before the clergyman, her husband-to-be mouthed words which she clearly understood: *You look lovely.* She desperately wanted him to find her so on this most special of days. Did he really think she looked pretty?

Even though there had been no time to procure a new gown, she had taken great pains with her appearance. A never-worn dress of ivory muslin as soft as a rose petal and much more thin was, to her mind, perfection. She wore satin slippers of ivory, and her only jewelry was her mother's pearl necklace.

When she had stood before her looking glass to

inspect her appearance, she was pleased to note her breasts looked rather womanly. Which is exactly how she wished to appear. Would de Vere notice?

Sensing her nervousness, he firmly clasped her hand and continued to hold it with firmness throughout the ceremony.

She turned back ever so slightly to catch a glimpse of her father, who sat on a gilded side chair a half a dozen feet away. Beneath his bushy white brows, his eyes glittered, and a self-satisfied smile settled on his lips.

Seeing her father so obviously happy caused her eyes to tear up, but she was in possession of just enough mastery over her emotions to keep from crying.

However, when de Vere vowed to take her for his wife, forsaking all others until death they did part, her composure crumbled once again.

That was when her . . . husband settled an arm around her and drew her closer to him. She found the protective gesture poignant.

When it was her turn to recite her vows to him, each word came out as a forlorn sob even though she was far from feeling forlorn.

It was not until the end of the ceremony that her tears receded. She looked up into de Vere's solemn face as it lowered to seal their vows with a kiss. Their first. Her first.

Suddenly she was filled with happiness. She was not only granting her father's fondest wish, she was also marrying the only man she could ever love. Her heart soared. The man she loved was now her husband.

While he was not without fault, she knew he was one of the most honest men in all of London.

If de Vere vowed to be a faithful husband, she knew he would not stray.

Now it was up to her to win his love.

It didn't seem right to be thinking of his bride's breasts during the solemn sacrament of matrimony, but doing so was the only way he could convince himself Miss Annabelle Pemberton was no longer Robert Pemberton's little girl but a full-grown woman who was now to be his own wife.

While waiting for her prior to the ceremony, he had become so nervous his limbs shook like the ground beneath a stampede of horses.

But then he saw her, saw how frightened she looked, and all thought of his own agitation disappeared. All that mattered to him was that he put . . . *his bride* at ease. It was dashed peculiar to think of himself as a husband, to think of Miss Pemberton as his wife.

She's no longer Miss Pemberton. Now she would be Lady de Vere. As his mother—God rest her soul—had been before her. The very notion of this tiny thing sharing his name, sharing his lands, sharing his life filled him with a buoyant sense of possession.

Following the ceremony, he continued to hold his wife's hand.

"Congratulations, my boy," Mr. Pemberton said, slapping him on the back. "It is my belief that one day you'll look back on this day and realize it was the luckiest day of your life. Come, let's have at that breakfast so you and my daughter can get on the road before the snows begin to fall."

Then Mr. Pemberton bent to kiss his

daughter's cheek. "You look radiant, love, or should I say, *my lady?*"

"Thank you, Papa. Have you reconsidered about joining us on the trip to Upper Barrington?" She looked up at her husband. "De Vere and I both would feel ever so much more happy if you would come with us."

He shook his head adamantly. "I told you, I'll come in a few days. I'll be there in plenty of time for Christmas."

De Vere's sister began to laugh. "Really, de Vere, your new father-in-law is right to decline. You and. . . may I still call you Belle?" Her gaze flicked to Belle.

"Certainly."

Charlotte turned back to her brother. "You and Belle need a few days to become accustomed to being man and wife."

De Vere regarded Charlotte with amusement. "Where has my maiden sister acquired such a breadth of knowledge about married persons?"

She glared at him. "I assure you, my knowledge of honeymoons was acquired at the same time I learned the alphabet."

They all laughed.

"I can well believe that," de Vere said, "owing to your insatiable interest in all things male."

"Before you depart," Robert Pemberton said to him when they sat down to a sumptuous breakfast, "I shall need you to sign the marriage contracts."

De Vere frowned. He exceedingly disliked having to discuss money with his former guardian. He hoped to God Pemberton did not think he was marrying Belle in order to get his hands on the Pemberton fortune.

While his bride changed into traveling clothes for their journey, he went with Pemberton to his library. "It gives me pleasure to know that I'm finally able to rescue my dear friend's lands," Pemberton said. "Like you, your father was too blasted proud to ever accept my financial help. I think I was even more upset than he when the roof collapsed on Hamptonworth."

De Vere frowned. "Because of my father's neglect."

"I know you're a much stronger man than he. I have no qualms at all that you'll gamble away my fortune."

"I give you my word that I won't."

"I know that you've always been a man of your word."

"A gentleman's word is his honor, and honor is something that can never be recovered, once lost." De Vere's eyes locked with the older man's. "You know I am not marrying Belle to get my hands on your wealth?"

Pemberton nodded. "I know. I also know you may not fancy yourself in love with Belle at present, but if I were given to wagering, I'd wager my entire fortune that you'll be in love with her—deeply in love with her—before your first wedding anniversary."

God, I hope he's right. "I have once again deferred to your wisdom."

"I had my man of business draw up the marriage contracts. Until my. . . passing, I have provided handsomely for you and my daughter—in case that physician is the idiot I've always thought him to be. In the event my death is not as imminent as that fool Marsden thinks, I wish to make certain that my daughter continues living in the manner in which she is accustomed. Therefore, you'll find the settlements more than generous. Then, of course, once I've gone, everything will come to you."

"It doesn't bother you that I will expect Belle to make her home at Hamptonworth instead of Upper Barrington?"

Pemberton shook his head. "Upper Barrington is merely a pup as far as houses go. I will own, I have pumped a great deal of money into it, but I think I always preferred the history and solidity of Hamptonworth. It's a national treasure. How old is it?"

"Almost four hundred years."

"I can't deny that I'm sorry I never had any sons to inherit Upper Barrington. I've spent most of my life trying to make it a grand country home. Throughout those years, though, I always thought one day Belle would marry a peer and become mistress of one of England's treasures. That's what I always wanted for her."

De Vere wasn't fool enough to believe this man merely wanted a title for his daughter. Pemberton wasn't that shallow. There was more to this wedding endorsement than was readily discernable.

Once de Vere signed the contracts and started for the door, Robert Pemberton called his name.

De Vere stopped and turned back to face his new father-in-law, his brow raised in query.

"You know she loves you?"

Belle? He gave a bitter laugh. A woman most certainly could not be in love with a man she so blatantly criticized at every opportunity. De Vere had no doubts Belle was marrying him solely to grant her father his last Christmas wish. He shrugged and left the chamber.

It was bitterly cold in the de Vere traveling coach. So cold, in fact, that the best way to keep from being completely miserable was to snuggle against one another for warmth. She had made certain that one large rug was warmed to ensure that they nestled beneath it for the two-hour journey to Upper Barrington.

As he held open the coach door for her, she gathered her velvet pelisse about her and climbed in. He entered, absently sitting across from her.

Her eyes flashing mischievously, she gave him a wicked smile and patted the seat beside her. "Dear Husband of Mine, I believe you'll be warmer sitting next to your wife. Besides, I have the rug, and I intend for us to share it."

He answered her with a grin and attempted to straighten his long body as he rearranged himself to sit beside her. In a most maternal fashion, she lifted the rug and covered both of them with it. She had deliberately not brought her muff. Without it to keep her hands warm, she hoped he would hold her hands instead. She did so excessively enjoy holding hands with this man she loved.

Once the rug had been thrown over them, she scooted as close to him as was possible. "Do you think we might hold hands?" she asked innocently.

He peered at her, his face solemn. "If you'd like."

She placed her hand into his. Though they both wore gloves, the fusion of their hands was incredibly intimate. Her gaze went to the outline of their thighs beneath the rug, side by side, his so long, hers so short. She realized she had never in her life been so close to a man. Her heart fluttered at the realization that this man was her husband. She gazed up at him.

"Warm?" he asked.

"As warm as is possible under the circumstances." Her gaze moved to the frosty carriage window and the bleak, gray skies beyond. She settled her face against his chest. "I do believe I'm going to like being married. It's nice to have someone with whom to. . . cuddle."

He began to laugh.

"What's so funny?"

"You."

"Why?"

"Because you're such an innocent."

She straightened. "You surely wouldn't wish to marry a woman who was not, would you?"

"I must own, until two days ago, I gave almost no thought to marrying *any* woman."

His words wounded. Must he so indirectly refer to the situation which precipitated this marriage? How she wished he could easily move on to the next chapter in their lives without dwelling on the last.

They settled into a strange silence, and she found herself wondering what kind of wife he would have selected, had he free choice. It was a most morose matter to contemplate. Of course, she would have been possessed of extraordinary beauty. And her family would have been one of the oldest, most respected in the kingdom. And, sadly, he would have loved her deeply.

What had she gotten herself into? Dare she hope de Vere would ever come to love her?

First, she had to ensure that he thought of her

as a woman. Perhaps she should not act the innocent. Would it even be possible for her act in another way? How did one become seductive? She was sadly ignorant of such matters.

Kissing had to be one of the components of being seductive. She could not deny she had excessively enjoyed the short kiss that concluded their wedding ceremony, and she most certainly hoped they could revisit such an activity.

"Do you think," she finally asked him, squeezing his hand that intertwined with hers, "I could call you *dearest*?"

He shrugged. "If you'd like."

She smiled. "Do you think perhaps we could kiss, too?"

He started laughing again.

She glared. How could a woman be seductive when the man she was attempting to seduce found her comical? "I see nothing funny about wanting to kiss one's husband."

"There is nothing funny about a husband and wife kissing. It's just that you are so very. . ." He peered down at her. "Cute, actually."

Since she could not aspire to great beauty, she thought she would be quite content to be considered *cute*. "I do hope you mean that in a good way."

Now he squeezed her hand. "I mean that in a good way."

"I have no objections if you should wish to call me by some affectionate term."

"Like *love*?"

That is how he had referred to her when she collapsed into tears before him. *Love*. It quite melted her heart. "I shall *love* it!"

He chuckled again.

"I am wondering if it is a good thing that one's husband finds her so amusing."

"Forgive me. It's just that I find you refreshing."

Not what she wanted to convey. She frowned. "Milk that comes straight from the cow is refreshing—but not what a bride wishes to be compared to."

"I do beg your forgiveness."

"It has occurred to me there are many things I don't know about you."

He turned to face her, and his handsomeness nearly stole away her breath. This close she could clearly see that the irises of his eyes were so deep a brown as to appear black. They were completely free of goldish flecks that were present in lighter irises.

Even the dark stubble where he had shaved that morning was easy to detect this close, as was his exotic musk scent. She fought the urge to press her finger into the deep cleft in his square chin.

He emanated such masculinity that she had the distinct feeling that were their coach stopped by highwaymen, her powerful husband could singlehandedly pummel every last one of them.

"Such as?" he asked.

"Children. I know you have admitted that you've given no thought to marriage. What about to children?"

"I find children delightful."

"Should you want sons or daughters?"

"It never occurred to me that I wouldn't have sons to take shooting and to teach all the things I learned from. . . your father."

Both of them grew solemn. Her father had not only been a wonderful father to her, he had served much as a father to de Vere as well. And their love for her father bound them to one another as surely as chains.

How they would miss him!

Once they were beyond the foggy environs of London, the landscape from their window was much lovelier, even if winter had stripped away all of its color. There was a certain peacefulness in the isolated little thatched cottages with smoke curling from their chimneys.

He still had difficulty believing he was a married man. Married to the tiny young woman who now sat beside him, her small hand resting within his, the tiny young woman he'd known most of his life. It would take time to become accustomed to marriage under any circumstances, and the haste under which this marriage—his marriage—had occurred made him feel as if he were rolling down a hill at breakneck speed.

Now he was reeling from her question about children. His children, to be precise. Something, some novel emotion, unfurled inside him when he spoke to Belle about having sons. It seemed almost incomprehensible that he would have sons with Belle. The very notion had him picturing sons who looked as Robert Pemberton had looked at fourteen when Gainsborough had painted him with his dog and musket. Only these young Robert Pembertons he pictured were short!

He found himself wondering of what stature Mrs. Pemberton had been, found himself wondering why he could not remember what the woman looked like. There had to be a portrait of her, but he had never noticed.

Then his thoughts came back to this marriage. He would be expected to share a bed with Belle, but blast it all, he could not contemplate such a thing!

Once again, he recalled her asking him to think of her breasts whenever he doubted she could be his wife. He visualized her as she had appeared strolling up to take her place beside him for the marriage ceremony. How lovely she had looked! The bodice of her gown dipped low enough in front to reveal the plump tops of her breasts. The vision had erased his conception that she was an eleven-year-old child. She was a grown woman. A woman with womanly breasts.

"I must say, Belle, this is the longest you've gone in a great while without finding something to criticize about me. Why is that?"

"I take vows seriously. This morning we pledged to become one flesh; therefore, I will try to never hurt you again. You are now part of me, and I shall be part of you."

Good Lord! The prospect was nearly terrifying. Nevertheless, he found himself patting her hand.

"Since you're to be my other half," she said, peering up at him, "I suppose I need to learn more about you. I don't mean those things men like to know about like how well you ride or stand your own with Gentleman Jackson or how fine a cricket player you are. I assure you, my knowledge of cricket is so lacking that I would not be able to determine who was good or who was bad at the sport."

He shrugged. "What else is there to know?"

"I shall endeavor to tell you what I do know about you. I know you're more bookish than others of your set."

He nodded. Was that something he should deny? Would women find such a trait less manly?

"I know that you value truth."

"That I am proud of."

"As you should be. I find truthfulness a most noble quality. Let me see, what else do I know about you? You're affectionate to your sisters."

He nodded. "It occurs to me I don't know a great deal about you."

"I share your love of books. What a grand marriage we'll have, sitting before the fire reading our respective books in complete silence!"

They both laughed.

"Let me guess as to your favorite authors." He made a great display of pinching at his clefted chin. "Shakespeare."

She nodded. "Of course. I adore him."

"I should think the tragedies."

She shook her head.

"The histories?"

She shook her head again.

A slow smile eased across his face. "The comedies! I confess I, too, prefer the comedies."

"I don't like any kind of tragedy."

She always had been soft hearted. "Then I suppose you like poetry."

"Of course. Can you guess which poets I admire?"

"Lord Byron. All the women adore him."

She shook her head. "He's lived his life so wickedly, I can't divorce the man from the poet. I refuse to read him anymore."

"Then I imagine you like the Lake Poets. Women like to worship nature."

"You'll find I'm not very modern in my poetic tastes. Though there is much to admire in

Wordsworth, Coleridge, and Southey, I look to the last century for my favorites."

It was the same with him. "Pope?"

She shook her head.

Dare he hope she felt the same affinity for Cowper as he did? It would be far too extraordinary. "Who, then?"

"Cowper."

He could not believe it! "How did you know he was my favorite?"

Her eyes widened. "I did not know it. What an extraordinary coincidence!"

Yes, it was. "Now, my lady, allow me to ask what you think about children."

"I adore them. I've always adored them. I love babies, and toddlers, and six-year-olds who've lost their front teeth, and nine-year-olds whose teeth are too big for their little faces. I suppose because I had no siblings, I always craved being around children who were younger than me."

"And do you prefer girls or boys?"

She grew solemn. "I had always hoped . . . my father would live to see a grandson." Her voice broke, her eyes misted.

He drew her close and planted soft kisses in her hair. "He may, love. He may."

She began to cough, separating from him, and turning her head away.

She had coughed a great deal on their journey, and it now seemed to him her cough had worsened. He turned to her, his brows lowered with concern. "How long have you been suffering that wretched cough?"

She shrugged. "It does seem a little worse each day."

"You should be snug in a warm room, not in

this frigid coach." He put his arm around her and gathered her close. "Perhaps you should put your face beneath the rug so the air you inhale won't be so cold to your compromised lungs."

Her little arm came around him as she nodded and nuzzled her face just below the rug that spread over their torsos. Soon she was asleep.

Hers was a surprisingly comforting presence but disappointingly different than he felt with others of her sex. A pity. With Belle, he felt protective, not seductive.

Chapter 5

"Put me down! I am not child!" She looked around to discover they had arrived at Upper Barrington under dim late afternoon skies. Her maddening husband was carrying her from the coach to the house as if she were a helpless babe.

She would almost rather he loathe her than to treat her so blasted fatherly.

He stopped in mid-stride and stood her up. "It's just that I hated to awaken you. You were sleeping so soundly, and that nasty cough has to be wearing on you." His gaze fanned over the gravel drive which was blanketed with a fresh snow. "I was trying to protect you from the cold."

She should be grateful for his concern, but she was not. He acted far too much like a father than a man who could ever come to desire physical intimacy with her. They silently trod to the massive front door of the equally massive house which looked far more like a medieval castle than a country home built during her father's lifetime. Her thoughts turned melancholy. *Will he ever desire me as a man desires a woman?*

She made up her mind on the spot she would not force this marriage. He would not be welcome in her bed until such time as she could be convinced that her bed was where he truly wanted to be. Up until this moment she has assumed she would give herself to him that very night, but now she knew it could be a very long time before this marriage would be consummated.

If it ever was.

Only a handful of servants stayed on at Upper Barrington year-round, the chief one being the housekeeper. She rushed to greet them, smashing her mobcap on her brown and silver curls. Belle understood that the middle-aged woman would have had no need to dress her hair since she'd been rattling around the big house almost alone for months.

Mrs. Farraday's quizzing gaze went first to de Vere.

"Lord de Vere," Belle said, "I should like to present our housekeeper, Mrs. Farraday." Turning to the woman, Belle added. "His lordship is my husband."

Her eyes wide with surprise, the bony Mrs. Farraday curtsied. Belle knew her marriage must be a shock to the housekeeper. Most people had assumed Miss Annabelle Pemberton was entrenched into spinsterhood.

Despite that de Vere was being beastly brotherly, Belle was rather overjoyed to be able to introduce this magnificent creature as her husband.

"Oh, dear me," Mrs. Farraday said, "I haven't prepared a room for his lordship. Will he be in yours, your ladyship?" The silly woman had wasted no time in addressing Belle by her new title. What was there about servants that made them so snobbish? All her servants back in London had swelled with pride to now be engaged by *a real lady* and wasted no time in addressing their mistress as such.

At the very idea of sharing her bedchamber with this man she had married, Belle's heartbeat roared. "The one next to mine, I should think." Somehow, she had managed to maintain her composure. She gazed up at de Vere and tried to speak casually. "Will that be agreeable to you, my darling?"

His dark eyes glittered. "A wise husband always defers to his wife's judgment."

He was likely thrilled not to have to sleep with her. *Odious man!*

"I'll have the room freshened up in just a few minutes," Mrs. Farraday reassured them. "And I'll see to it that a nice fire's built in each chamber."

While they waited for the fires to warm their personal chambers, Belle whisked him about the common areas of the big, chilly house to refresh him on the floor plan. They soon went to their chambers to change for dinner, which would be served at five o'clock—total darkness at this time of the year. She was looking forward to the peaceful hours kept in the country.

They climbed the broad brick stairway, her hand skimming along its solid Romanesque banister that could compete with the ancient statuary that was scattered throughout the house and grounds. On the third floor, they stopped at the first chamber in the corridor: hers. She was conscious of feeling awkward standing there in front of its closed door.

"I'll collect you at five," he said. To her astonishment, he bent to kiss her.

On the cheek. *Odious man!*

At five, she awaited just behind her chamber door, quickly opened it upon his knock, and began to step into the corridor when she noticed the red velvet box in her husband's hand.

He cleared his throat. "I wanted to bring you this necklace from the de Vere jewels. Thought you might wish to wear it to dinner."

Her face lifted into a smile. "That would be lovely!" She backed into the chamber, widening the door for him. "Allow me to look at it where the light is better." When she stood beside her French dressing table, which was lighted by a pair of torchieres on either side, he handed her the box. Its crimson velvet had long ago faded to where it now resembled a rose blush.

She tried to remember the late Lady de Vere wearing jewels, but she was too young when that lady had died. She eased open the hinged top and was dazzled at the beauty of the multi-layered diamond necklace. Her breath hitched.

Her first thought was that she wished she had known the necklace was coming so she could have selected a gown that would display it as something that beautiful should be displayed, but she did not want to say anything that would make him think she was not honored to wear his family jewels. "Oh, my lord! It's magnificent!"

She was not exaggerating for his benefit. Despite all her father's riches, neither she nor her mother had ever possessed anything so beautiful. Her eyes—lamentably—misted. Why did everything this man did have such a profound effect upon her emotions? She looked up at him. "Will you fasten it upon me?"

"May I suggest you sit at the dressing table?"

She lowered herself to the gilt and velvet chair and sat there peering into the glass, as he settled the gems high on her chest and clasped them behind her neck. The scalloped rows of large diamonds descended to the center where the largest of the diamonds poised just above the separation of her breasts. One could not gaze upon the necklace without seeing her bosom.

She and her maid—whose carriage arrived at Upper Barrington just after the bride and groom—had taken great care with her appearance, her first dinner as Lady de Vere. The blue velvet gown was favored for two reasons, the first being that it matched her eyes, which were said to be her best feature.

The other reason for donning the gown was that its neckline was cut so low, it displayed her breasts to great advantage. Despite that she was small of stature, her breasts were not small. Surely, that was a good thing. Did men not admire women with full breasts? *Would de Vere even notice?*

Her dress also favorably displayed a large expanse of milky shoulders, and the combination of smooth, pale skin, blue velvet, and glittering diamonds was the closest thing to perfection that had ever appeared in her looking glass. She could not have selected a gown better suited to display the de Vere diamonds.

"I am destitute of words to tell you how beautiful it is, how honored I am to wear it."

He watched her reflection, his face serious. "I am destitute of words to tell you how lovely you are. You have never looked prettier."

His words had her feeling like a diamond, sparkling from the inside out. "Oh, my lord, that is exceedingly kind of you. I am so touched that with all you've had to do these past two days, you thought of me."

"What's this *my lord* about? You're not one of my servants."

She swallowed. "No. I'm your wife. I've the de Vere jewels to prove it!" She stood, and he crooked his arm to escort her to dinner.

After dinner they came to the lofty library, a long room of soaring ceilings with dark, book-lined walls and real wood fires blazing in scattered inglenooks throughout the chamber. He quite thought it was his favorite room in all of England. "You must not be offended," he teased, "when I tell you that this library was a very strong recommendation for marrying you."

She smiled. "You always did love this room. That is something else we have in common. It's my favorite room, too. Should you like to select a book?" Her gaze climbed up to the catwalk that circled the upper storey of the library.

"Where shall I begin?"

"I could direct you. What would like to read? Cowper?"

He shook his head. "No. I'm in the mood for something serious. Someone like Burke."

"Come right this way."

He followed her past nearly a dozen bookcases filled with fine leather and gilt books. "Here." She paused in front of a case filled mostly with Burke's writing. He also spotted volumes of nonfiction by Charles Lamb, Jeremy Bentham, Edward Gibbons, and Rousseau. "Papa has two shelves of Burke's discourses. I daresay every word ever written by the man can be found here."

"Our fathers were not just his friends but also his admirers. We, too, have all his works at Hamptonworth, and I'm in the process of reading every one of them."

She picked up one slim volume with a heavily

scrolled cover titled *Burke's Speech on Conciliation with America*. "No matter which of his works I read, I continue to marvel at his exceptional eloquence, marvel that I actually spoke to the man once."

"I know of no man who can write with more sense, and of course you're right about the eloquence." He took the book. "I haven't read this one. I have now in my hands a few hours of reading pleasure."

She selected another book from the same shelf. "We have found still another author upon whom we perfectly agree." She linked her arm through his. "Come let us go read."

They settled in a cozy alcove on a velvet settee in front of a fire. A tall window on their right was draped in emerald colored silk.

"I love to read here on a frigid winter day," she told him, her voice soft. "This window is the only one which offers us a wonderful view of Capability Brown's lake." As soon as she spoke, her cough commenced.

His brows lowered. "Are you all right?"

It was a moment before she could respond, a minute before her nasty cough subsided. Then she merely nodded.

Not five minutes later, she went into another coughing fit. He did not like the sound of it, but then he could never hear a female coughing and not be reminded of his mother's final weeks, when consumption stole away the last of her last breaths. With each successive cough from Belle, a melancholy agitation mounted within him.

This time when she stopped, he got up and rang for a servant.

"What are you doing?" she asked.

"You know very well what I'm doing."

"Allow me to rephrase. Why are you summoning a servant?"

"Because I wish to procure a shawl to drape about you to ward off the chill. And I think you need a glass of warm milk."

"Honestly, de Vere, I wish you would not treat me like I'm your child!"

"I don't think you should address me as de Vere now that we're married. It's what all the bloods call me."

She peered up at him, and he was powerless not to gaze at her breasts dipping beneath the blue velvet, powerless not to consider how much he would enjoy peeling away that blue velvet. "How would you like me to refer to you?" she asked, her voice low.

"My name's William."

"I'm well aware of that fact. It's the name I called you until you succeeded when I was eleven."

He frowned. "I was not happy when you suddenly began to call me de Vere like everyone else."

"You objected to being called by your title?"

He shrugged. "At first it seemed like I was stealing my father's name. It didn't seem to fit me. Far too stuffy for a lad still three years away from obtaining his majority. I thought it far too . . . cold and impersonal."

Her eyes misted. "I wish I'd known. . . I would have continued to call you William. I remember how melancholy you appeared to me, how hard I prayed for you that year."

He doubted anyone had ever prayed for him in his life. A single brow elevated. "You prayed for me?"

She nodded. "I worried so about you having no parent, about you having to grow up practically overnight. I cannot tell you how keenly my heart ached for you."

"You were surely the only person in the kingdom who did not think me fortunate."

"Then the others didn't know you as I like to think I did."

A warmth spread throughout his body. There *was* an intimacy between him and this woman he had married, an intimacy that stretched back for many years now. How could he have failed to acknowledge it long before now?

The butler entered the chamber, and de Vere dispatched him for the shawl and milk.

"So you really thought I was cold and impersonal when I quit calling you William?"

Their eyes locked.

"Can you deny it? You've betrayed more emotion in the past eight and forty hours than you have in the past twelve years."

She spoke solemnly. "I was schooled that to be a proper lady, I needed to be an elegant icicle."

"Then, my lady, you were an apt pupil." He fleetingly thought about reminding her that his sisters had continued to call him William after he succeeded, but he knew she did not want to be linked with his sisters—and not because she wasn't on terms of intimacy with each of them.

For the first time, he could honestly say he no longer thought of her quite like he thought of his sisters. Yet it wasn't the same as it had been with his inamoratas, either. He did have to acknowledge —if only to himself—he and Belle had progressed to an uncommon hinterland over the past four and twenty hours, but it was still bloody difficult to believe Belle was his wife. He still was not comfortable with the realization he was a married man, a man married to a woman with whom he was not in love.

Some ten minutes passed before the butler returned with a glass of warm milk and a bright red Kashmir shawl. As if she were a complete invalid, De Vere took the items, setting the milk down on a table beside her, then proceeding to drape the shawl about her bare shoulders. "Here, love. As pretty as your gown is, it offers little protection against the chill to your delicate body."

And he needed to cover up that damn necklace that drew attention to her breasts like an arrow to its target.

"I do wish you would not think of me as so decidedly delicate." A subsequent coughing spell belied her words.

Each harrowing cough reminded him of his poor mama.

Though it angered her that he would coddle her in the same way as would a brother—or, worse yet, a father—there was no way she could remain angry with a man who treated her with such deep concern.

As long as her coughing intruded on their silent reading, her bridegroom was incapable of concentrating on his book. She needed to engage him in conversation. She lay her book in her lap. "William?"

A slow, bone-melting smile eased across his handsome face as he looked up at her, a nearly black brow cocked.

"You must share with me your plans for

Hamptonworth. I'm greatly looking forward to making our home there."

"I had no idea you father was so attached to the place. Now, due to his generosity with the wedding settlement, needed improvements can be made."

"For which I am as happy as Papa."

A troubled look passed over his face. "I would never want you to think. . ."

"I know you would never marry for fortune. Don't ever believe I would think that."

"Good. Because I'd give away Hamptonworth before I'd marry for money."

"I do understand that."

He leaned back and stared into the roaring wood fire. "It will cost a small fortune to make all the repairs that are necessary."

"Do you plan to do anything new there?"

"If engaging a complete gardening staff which we haven't had for more than a decade is considered something new, then yes."

"I'm so happy to hear that. I can only barely remember sitting in the rowboat on Hamptonworth's lake surrounded by all those lovely walks, all the beautiful flowers, the well-trimmed shrubberies and sculpted trees."

He nodded. "I vividly remember that, too, but the place has become overgrown and unkempt in recent years. I haven't allowed visitors to witness its demise."

She averted her gaze. "So I've heard. I'm so happy we're going to bring it back. It will be a wonderful place for our childr- - -" What was she saying? How forward she was being! What happened to her resolve to make him *want* to come to her bed? The last thing she wanted was for him to feel compelled to make love with her. She quickly shook her head. "Honestly, I don't want to rush things between us."

"There will be time. I, too, have no desire to force what should occur naturally."

Her cheeks stung. She was trying to determine if he had just repelled her or not.

Then she was once more overcome by a coughing fit.

He drew her hand within his own. Her chest expanded. "It's been a long, eventful day," he said when she stopped coughing, "and now, my dear, you need nothing more than a good night's sleep." He handed her the glass of milk. "Drink up."

As they climbed the stairs to their bedchambers, she realized he was right. She *was* uncommonly tired. He was right, too, about her wellbeing. She wasn't really feeling quite the thing.

Her heart raced, but she wasn't sure if that was not owing to the fact she had never before held hands with a gentleman in such an intimate fashion. For those few fleeting moments, she thought she knew what it must feel like to be cherished by a man.

The corridor on the bedchamber floor was only dimly lit from a scattering of wall scones, and the candle had burnt out in one of those, the one beside her door. They both came to a stop there.

He stood so close, she could feel his heat, smell his musky scent. She lifted her face, and he lowered his head to kiss her.

This time it was *not* a peck on the check. His arms came fully around her, and she hugged him close as the kiss deepened, as their mouths opened to each other, intensifying the connection between.

When the magical kiss was over, he spoke in a husky voice. "I assure you that is *not* how I kiss my sisters."

Still unconsciously stroking the angular planes of his beloved face, she nodded. She was still too breathless to speak, too stunned to speak without her voice trembling like her entire body already was.

A moment later she said, "I pray you don't catch my cold."

He ran a seductive finger down the length of her pert nose. "I would have no regrets." Then he turned to stride to his chamber.

CHAPTER 6

He dreamt that his mother was still alive. But she was dying with each hacking cough. He jerked awake and sat up. Total darkness surrounded him because the heavy velvet curtains closed around his bed. It took a moment before he came fully awake and realized his mother had been buried many years ago. The anguish of her drawn-out death flared anew, and his melancholy spread like spilled ink.

Good God, had Bell's coughing awakened him? He sat completely still, holding his breath, afraid that his own breathing would obscure the sounds from her room.

Nothing.

How foolish he'd been! A house built by the staggeringly wealthy Mr. Pemberton would have walls so thick one could scarcely hear a cannon were it fired in the next room.

Attempts to return to sleep failed. At dawn, he rose and tried to read Burke, but his worries about Belle mounted. A frown etching into his face, he began to pace the chamber's soft broadloom carpet. Damn, he'd been married but one day, and its effects were already wearing on him.

What had he gotten himself into?

A pity he was powerless to push away his melancholy thoughts. He kept picturing Belle as his mother had looked when last he'd seen her in the coffin. He would know no peace until he saw Belle with his own eyes, saw that she was her delightful self.

At midmorning, they met in the drawing room. Relief rushed over him. She looked perfectly fit—even if he could not approve of what she wore. That thin pale blue muslin that exposed much of her arms and chest would offer little protection against a chill. Did she have no more sense than to dress in such a way? It was if she were inviting lung fever!

Oddly enough, he no longer thought of her as a girl. She suddenly looked like a woman. He even found himself happily observing her womanly breasts. Without guilt. After all, she *had* encouraged him to do so. "How are you feeling today?" he asked.

She helped herself to a cup of hot tea. "Much better since I had my morning tea."

"How did you sleep?"

"Wretchedly. Do you know of a cure for coughing?"

He went to ring for a servant. "Aqua cordials. I'm going to request one for you."

Before he reached it, their butler entered the chamber with a silver tray bearing but a single card. "For you, my lady."

De Vere thought the young man just might have what it takes to be a good butler. Belle had elevated one of her father's footmen to the post, and he had arrived at Upper Barrington the previous day, along his wife's maid and his own valet.

Belle read the name on the card, and her face brightened. "Show him in!"

"Who, my love, are you showing in?" de Vere

inquired once the footman left the chamber.

"My friend and neighbor, Sir George Bennington. Do you know him?"

He shook his head.

A moment later, the neighbor came striding into the room with an insufferably proud bearing. The man's height may have exceeded de Vere's, and de Vere was a couple of inches over six feet. Sir George was likely closer to Belle's age, probably five and twenty. He dressed as a well-tailored country gentleman with his fine woolen jacket hugging his narrow waist, buff breeches, and soft brown leather boots. Too fine for de Vere's taste. Everything—even his hair—was some variation on the same shade of medium brown, the ivory of his linen shirt the only thing breaking up the monochromatic look.

The man was incapable of disguising his deep affection for de Vere's wife. Had his appreciative gaze been confined to Belle's face, de Vere might have looked more favorably upon the intruder, but the man had the audacity to whisk his shimmering gaze over *de Vere's wife's* body!

She had risen when he entered the chamber and happily rushed to him, offering her hand to be kissed. "It's been an age since we've seen each other!" she exclaimed.

"Far too long." He continued to hold her hand as he sensed they were not alone. "You and your father have come for Christmas?"

"Papa will arrive soon." She turned slightly away, facing de Vere. "Sir George, I must make you known to my husband."

Were the man a pup, his wagging tail would have stilled. The smile completely disappeared from his face.

And for the first time, de Vere was proud to stand up and say he was a married man. Not that he really *wanted* to be married to anyone. He rose and glared at Sir George while his wife facilitated the introductions.

The visitor grumbled a salutation, then directed his attention at Belle. "I had no inkling you were getting married! When did this occur?" He did not sound happy.

She bestowed a smile upon the newcomer. "We married yesterday."

"Oh, dear me. I don't suppose you and your father will be gathering holly up at Happy Hill Farm now."

De Vere moved close to his wife and set a protective hand to her waist. "My wife is nursing a nasty cough. I'm not allowing her out of doors until we see improvement." He smiled down at her.

Sir George's eyes narrowed as he glared at de Vere. "*You're* not allowing her?" His angry gaze flicked to Belle. "Since when have you ever let anyone dictate to you? Why even your own father always said no one could tell his daughter- - -"

"Now, now, Sir George," she chided, "dear de Vere is merely concerned over my welfare. I assure you he's not at all the ogre you must think him."

"I am deeply concerned over *my* wife's wellbeing." Now de Vere's eyes narrowed.

"Come, gentlemen," Belle said, "let us sit down. I am so looking forward to you two getting to know one another."

De Vere was quite sure he could die happy without ever having to get to know the man who so obviously had eyes for *his* wife. He stayed as close as a shadow as she went to a silken sofa, and when she sat, he sat next to her. Close. For good measure, he drew her hand into his. Show that demmed baronet the former Miss Annabelle Pemberton was now a married woman!

The baronet's civility restored, he peered at de Vere and spoke in a more calm voice. "So you're the Lord de Vere of Hamptonworth Hall?"

"I am."

"I cannot believe the two of you have never met since you've been my two best male friends all of my life."

De Vere did not know why Belle ever needed any other male companions when she had him.

"Wasn't your father his guardian?"

"Yes, indeed. Our fathers were lifelong best friends."

If de Vere was not mistaken, Sir George gulped. "Then you've always known each other?"

De Vere smiled down at his wife. "You might say we, too, have always been best friends."

She looked up adoringly at him. He had not known Belle was so accomplished an actress. "And then the friendship deepened, and here we are!"

His head lowered to brush a kiss across her cheek. "And I am the most fortunate man in the kingdom." He wasn't such a bad actor himself.

Then his wife's wretched coughing returned. Each hack was like the slice of a knife through his own flesh. He couldn't stand to hear it. He got up and stormed to the bell pull to summon the servant for the aqua cordial he'd forgotten to request in Belle's excitement over her caller. The servant promptly came, and de Vere sent him off to fetch what he hoped would be a restorative for his poor, hacking wife.

"I see what you mean, de Vere, about Miss Pemberton's nasty cough."

DeVere stiffened. "Lady de Vere, if you will."

"Sorry." Sir George eyed Belle. "Your father always did want you to marry a peer."

"Unlike my dear father, I don't care a fig about titles." Once again she adoringly looked up at him. Even though he knew it was all a bluff, his insides tightened and his chest seemed to expand. "I'm quite sure I would have fallen in love with de Vere were he a . . . a country solicitor!"

He thought of Pemberton's comment. *She loves you, you know?* He hadn't believed it for a moment. Still didn't. But when she acted as she was acting now, it etched those words so deep in his memory, it was impossible to suppress them.

As he gazed down into his wife's face filled with mock adoration, he was nearly overcome with a strong desire to kiss here. Not a brush across the cheek, but a deep, wet, hungry kiss. Which he couldn't do as long as Sir George was sitting there staring at them.

She pulled her gaze away from him. "But that's enough about us, Sir George. You must tell me, are your brothers and sisters coming for Christmas?"

He shook his head solemnly. "None of my sisters. They're all busy filling their nurseries. Freddie, though, will come. He should arrive tomorrow. I would have waited until he came to call on you but, but when I saw your carriage drive past the farm yesterday, I knew you'd be here, and I was impatient to see you."

Cheeky blade!

"It has been an age since I've been here, since I

last saw you." She shrugged. "I know one pines away for good company here in the country—and what I mean by good company is the companionship of dear, old friends."

"That is true. So true, my lady. I suppose I should spend more time in Town, but you know I'm happiest shooting and such."

She nodded, then eyed her husband. "Sir George is not enamored of London life."

"Then that explains why we haven't previously met."

The servant bought the aqua cordial in a slender glass, handing it to de Vere. "Here, love, drink up," he told his wife. He wished like the devil he had a shawl to drape around her shoulders, to keep off the chill.

And to keep Sir George's hungry gaze off *his* wife's bosom.

Once again, de Vere got up and stormed to the bell pull.

"Now why are you summoning Robertson?" she asked when she put down her drink.

"He needs to fetch your shawl. Have you, my lady, looked out the window? Snow is all over the ground! You're not dressed nearly warm enough—especially for one whose health is already so compromised!"

Even as he spoke, de Vere saw Sir George's lascivious gaze lower to Belle's very fine breasts.

When Robertson came, Belle told him where to find her shawl.

"In addition to the aqua cordial," Sir George said, "I have found chamomile tea aids in suppressing coughs."

Belle nodded. "I did notice that after my morning tea, my cough seemed to improve."

When the servant entered the room with the Kashmir shawl, de Vere dispatched him to the kitchen for chamomile tea.

"Make that for three," Belle said.

Sir George stood. "None for me, thank you. I must be going."

"So soon?" Belle sounded disappointed.

"I have many things to see to before Freddie arrives. I merely wanted to say hello—and invite you over, but under the circumstances, what with your nasty cough and all, Lord de Vere's right to keep you indoors."

Lord and Lady de Vere rose to bid their visitor farewell. Once he was gone, Belle's honeyed gazes were quickly replaced with a sour lemon expression. "I am excessively embarrassed over your hostility to my dear friend."

"I wasn't hostile."

"You most certainly were!"

"In what way?"

She thought on it for a moment. "Your facial expressions. You *glared* at him! It wouldn't have hurt you to crack a smile or to tell him it was nice to make his acquaintance—neither of which you did."

Just thinking about that. . .that *neighbor* made him glare again. "If you must know, I didn't care for the fellow."

"That was obvious, and you have no reason whatsoever to feel that way. I assure you, Sir George is the sweetest man possible."

What man wants to be thought of as "sweet"? "Especially to *my* wife! Has it never occurred to you that man is in love with you?"

"Oh, that!" She shrugged. "There is the fact he once proposed marriage to me, but I couldn't possibly marry a man I think of as a brother." As soon as the words were out of her mouth, a sadness swept over her face.

Was she remembering that just a few days ago he told her he thought of her as a sister? He'd had no idea that his brotherly affection was so repellant to her. Could that possibly mean . . .? Mr. Pemberton's words intruded again. Could she possibly have married him because she *was* in love with him?

"And one more thing!" She was still out of charity with him. "You come across as being a dictatorial, overbearing, obtuse husband, ordering me about as if I were some errant child."

"You're just angry because you think I act fatherly when what you really want is a doting lover, and I'm not that man!" Good lord! He'd raised his voice to her—something he'd never before done. And he'd said something cruel, to boot. But he was not in a good humor. And it was all her fault.

All because he had taken the irrevocable leap into matrimony.

Now she was the one doing the glaring. "Then why are you so jealous of Sir George?"

Jealous? Him? "If I were a jealous man—which I'm not!—Sir George is the last man in the kingdom I'd envy." He stormed from the chamber, muttering. *"Sweet! What man wants to be sweet?"*

He had hurt her when he said he couldn't be her doting lover. It had been difficult for her to fight back the tears, but Belle was too proud to allow him to know how really vulnerable she was, how close he had come to the truth.

In her emotional distress, the intensity of her

coughing strengthened. She poured herself more hot chamomile tea, oblivious to the tears that spilled into her cup.

Alone, her thoughts turned to . . . William. Thinking of de Vere by his Christian name gave her a comforting warmth. There was consolation in the fact no other woman in the kingdom—except for his sisters—could call the devilishly handsome man she had married by his first name.

It was very small consolation for having married a man who could never love her.

As her coughs subsided and her tears dried, she remembered how delighted she had been when she had thought William might be jealous of Sir George. Even if she had been angry with him.

He had been right about one thing. It was too cold for her to venture out of doors—at least as long as this nasty cough lingered.

How much more satisfying it would be to sit reading in the library's nook before a crackling fire, the lovely view of Upper Barrington's winter landscape glimpsed from the nearby window.

She went there straightaway.

Only to find the room was already occupied by her maddening husband. As she entered, he looked up from the book he was reading. "Forgive me if I've taken your favorite spot, but you were right about the view from here. It's difficult to concentrate on one's reading with so much loveliness beckoning."

He no longer sounded angry. "There's room enough for two—if I'm not intruding on you." She spoke stiffly.

"Not at all."

She picked up the same book she'd been

reading the night before and went to sit on the sofa where he sat, but several feet away from him. Not at all like they had sat when Sir George had called and she had flattered herself that William had been jealous.

For half an hour they read in silence. Not that she could have explained a single word written by the normally erudite Edmond Burke. Her mind kept racing over the confrontation she'd had with her husband, and she felt wretched over it. Had she been the didactic one? How did a marriage of four and twenty hours give her the right to tear into him? The more she dwelt on their cross words, the lower she became. Any misgivings he already harbored about his marriage would be magnified tenfold now. Now that he'd come to realize he'd married a self-centered, spoiled only child who was accustomed to having things her own way. What could she do to undo the harm?

Robertson entered the chamber. "A package has been sent to your father, my lady, and I thought you might like to see it."

He held a small box wrapped in string. It looked to be the size that would accommodate a jar of pickles. "Has it come from a Mrs. Blaine-Ramsbury of Edgemont Farm?"

The butler peered at the box. "Indeed it has, my lady."

"Then it's Cousin Betsy's pickles. No doubt she's sent them to Papa for Christmas. Please take them to the kitchen."

The butler's diversion gave her the break from reading she needed to address her husband. Gripped by remorse, she flung aside her book and addressed him. "Pray, William, can you possibly forgive me for my shrewish outburst?" She hoped that by calling him his Christian name she could establish some degree of intimacy.

He quickly discarded his book and faced her, his black eyes shimmering with warmth, so different than they'd been when he'd stormed from the drawing room. "It's I who should be asking for forgiveness." He scooted closer and drew her hand into his. "I'm beastly sorry for the way I spoke to you. And I apologize, too, for my shameful conduct to your *sweet* friend."

They both broke out laughing.

"I still don't like him," de Vere snapped.

"I assure you, he's perfectly sweet."

"About the jealousy. . . I've never been jealous, but I am possessive."

Her breathing hitched. He felt possessive toward her! Surely that was a good thing. She nodded, her heartbeat thumping in her chest.

"I admit I don't like a not-unattractive baronet making a cake of himself over *my* wife."

She tried to imagine how she would feel if an attractive woman threw herself at William. And a smile leapt to her lips. She would have quickly latched on to him as close as pages in a book. Which is exactly what her husband had done!

She scooted even closer. "I'm sure I would have felt the same, were the tables turned."

Her comment obviously made him uncomfortable for he looked away, his gaze captured by the solitary scene out the window. "I'm reminded of Christmases at Hamptonworth Hall."

"I hope we can be there next Christmas," she said, her voice soft. "I believe the view from its folly overlooking the lake is one of the most beautiful scenes in all of England. I do believe I'd rather be there than anywhere else."

His eyes widened. "I feel the same."

So they really did have a great many things in common. Was that not a good foundation upon which to build a marriage? But what of love, she thought, dejected. She definitely needed to divert the trajectory of her grim thoughts. "You mustn't think I wed you in order to be mistress of Hamptonworth just because I prefer it over any property in the three kingdoms."

"And with your fortune, my Lady de Vere, it will be beautiful once again."

She did adore being addressed as Lady de Vere. "William?"

He gazed at her, his eye flicking to the shawl which had begun to slip from her shoulder. He tenderly settled it close to her neck. "Yes?"

"When will we be able to go there? How I would love to once again see Hamptonworth in the winter."

"We will, love. We could have gone directly from here, but I thought you'd not want to be leaving your father."

Her shoulders sank. For the past hour she'd been able to forget the heartbreaking reality that her father was dying. She sighed. "You're right. I will not leave Papa."

Her husband quickly changed the subject. "Your cough has improved."

She was touched that he'd redirected the conversation away from so melancholy a topic, touched over his obsession over her cough. "It must be that aqua cordial you practically forced down my throat!"

"I take my husbandly duties seriously."

"What wifely duties can I fulfill?" She solemnly

looked up into his face.

Just as his head lowered to hers. . .

Chapter 7

His mouth greedily claimed hers as he swept her into his arms like a hungry predator. To his astonishment, her arms came fully around him, and the potency of her kiss matched the passion of his. He was powerless to lighten his touch, powerless to ease his crushing hold on this delicate woman. Any grip he'd had on rational thought fled under the onslaught of the intense emotions that consumed him. He was completely submerged in the thundering of his own heart, the sweet, low whimpers low in her throat, the debilitating need that strummed through every cell in his body.

When he recovered enough to loosen his hold, he peered down into her face. It was a face ravaged by the vestiges of passion.

Such an intoxicating vision was like throwing kindling upon his fire. As she pressed sultry circles into the muscles of his back, he began to trace a path of wet butterfly kisses along the smooth curve of her elegant neck. And lower.

When he realized what he was trying to do to the innocent he had married, he bolted up. "You must forgive me," he managed, his voice still husky and uneven. "I don't know what I was thinking." He leapt to his feet, his hands curled into balls.

Her voice trembled when she spoke. "You have no need to apologize. I am you wife, William."

He felt so blasted guilty, he couldn't look her in the eye. "If you will forgive me, my lady, I have to sort out a few things." He turned his back on her and strode to the door.

What the hell had he been thinking? With his fists still balled, he raced across the cold stone floors of the hall, snatched his greatcoat from the cloak room, and stormed from the house. His boots made indentations in the crunchy snow as he ambled toward the stables that were located a couple of hundred yards behind the big house. What he needed was a good, bruising ride.

Less than ten minutes later, he was astride one of his former guardian's fine stallions and galloping across the carpet of snow that rose and dipped according to the terrain. As fine a property as Upper Barrington was, it wasn't Hamptonworth. How he wished to be there at the family home where he'd spent every Christmas of his life. It was the home where he hoped to raise his family.

His family? Since when had the dissolute William Addison, Viscount de Vere, wanted a family? He had never really given the matter much consideration before. Before he learned Robert Pemberton was dying. Before he married Belle. Before he found himself desiring her as a man desires a woman.

The very memory of holding her in his arms was so indelible he could not purge himself of the continuing pleasure it gave. It was so different from any other physical encounter with any other woman, he was utterly perplexed. He tried telling himself different was not necessarily bad, just perplexing.

His horse pounded across the snow-covered

valley where the only things visible were white slopes and tall, barren trees laced with white against the soft brown of their trunks. So befuddled was he over these novel feelings he was experiencing, he was not even conscious of the cold, not conscious that the snow had begun to come down again, much heavier even than on the previous night.

As he rode, the sky darkened. Because of his own stormy countenance, he did not notice that, either. It seemed like an affirmation of his mood.

Why in the blazes was he so awkward about this intimacy with Belle? It wasn't as if he hadn't passionately kissed a woman before. But Belle, he realized, wasn't just another woman. Belle was now his wife. Belle was a woman to be cherished. Good Lord! Belle was the woman who would bear his children.

That simple explanation cleared his murky thoughts. Belle was not only his wife. Belle was to be his life's partner. And suddenly such a prospect no longer annoyed. Had he looked over the entire kingdom, never could he have found a woman better suited to him.

She loved Hamptonworth in the same way he loved it. She was attracted to the same authors he was. They moved in the same circles and shared many friends. She was possessed of keen intelligence. In addition, she was loving and generous and was kind to her servants. Her pretty face had become his obsession, and her petite body, his lingering aphrodisiac. But most important of all, they were friends.

He thought of what he'd told Sir George earlier that day. He and Belle were lifelong best friends. Which was true—though he hadn't realized it when he'd sniped at Sir George.

Sir George! Now de Vere realized the veracity of his wife's accusation. He *was* jealous of Sir George in the same way he would resent any man who was in love with *his* wife.

He quickly turned around his horse. He needed to behold Belle, the woman with whom he had fallen in love. The acknowledgement that he was in love with her was as liberating as coming out of shackles.

But could she possibly return his feelings? He remembered her father's words. Could she really be in love with him? He remembered the way she had kissed him with such intensity. No one could feign a response like that. Then he remembered her face as it looked when he last beheld her. Those heavy-lidded eyes were as sultry as a tropical night.

The very memory sent a surge of heat bolting through him even though his cheeks were red from the frost, his hands shivering from the piercing cold. His hunger to see her, to declare himself to her, propelled him like an Atlantic gale. He went straight to the front door of Upper Barrington and handed off the reins to a young footman who wore the Pemberton scarlet livery.

And there in the doorway stood Belle, the red Kashmir shawl swaddled around her, a forlorn look on her sweet face. "I've been so worried about you! Look at how dark it's gotten. I was afraid you would get stranded and . . . freeze to death."

A gleam in his eye, he came to her and set a gentle hand at her waist. "Back to the library, my love. We need to talk."

They returned to the same sofa where they had shared the passionate kiss. Though there were some eight different velvet sofas in the chamber, he would forevermore think of this one as theirs.

She sat, her face solemn as she eyed him.

He fell to his knees before her and drew her hand into his.

Then a knock sounded upon the library door. He grimaced, annoyed.

"Yes? You may come in," she answered in an elevated voice.

What would the servant think if he saw his master on his knees? De Vere quickly moved to the sofa, close to Belle.

Robertson strode into the chamber. "A letter arrived for you about an hour ago, my lady. Since it's from your father, Mrs. Farraday thought you might want to see it before you examined the rest of the day's post."

"Indeed I do." She took the letter and began to read.

De Vere watched as her expression became as solemn as one reading Scripture in church. Then she began to softly weep.

"Whatever it is, my dearest love," he said tenderly, "we can face it together."

She looked up from the paper in her hand, and a stupendous smile brightened her face. "It's good news! See, read for yourself." She handed him the letter from her father.

My Dearest Belle,

I am quickly writing this to ease your mind. I have only this day realized that Marsden is the fool I've always taken him for. I am not dying! I have discovered—much to my disappointment—that I can no longer eat Cousin Betsy's delicious pickles. Every time I eat one, I suffer the most severe pains in my chest. Two days ago I snapped to the correlation between the pickles and the pains; after your wedding, I put my theory to the test, and I experienced severe chest pain within minutes of eating one of Betsy's pickles. Consultation with others of my age has convinced me that as one ages, one is not always able to continue eating the same things one enjoyed when younger. Lord Sefton admitted he has been forced to give up broccoli, which causes him chest discomfort now, though he has eaten great amounts of it throughout his life.

I will arrive at Upper Barrington on Christmas Eve so that we may all celebrate Christ's birthday—and my continued good health—together at St. Stephen's on Christmas morning. We have much for which to be thankful.

I hope you and your husband are becoming acquainted as a loving couple is expected to do on their honeymoon. I fully expect de Vere to be the doting husband by the time I arrive.

De Vere dropped the note. "I am."

She eyed him skeptically. "You are what?"

"Your devoted husband." His voice was raw when he continued. "I've come to realize I'm in love with you. I will do anything in my power to win your affection."

"There is nothing you can do now to win my affection."

His face fell, but not as thuddingly as his heart.

Her blue eyes flashed with mirth. "Because you already possess it."

He drew both her hands into his. "Truly?"

She nodded. "Always. I have loved you since I was a little girl and dreamed of growing up and marrying my dear William."

"I am your William, your slave, your eternal conquest." His arms then closed around her, and she fused to him like bark to a tree.

"It's already dark, my dearest," she whispered. "Do you think we can go upstairs?"

"I can think of nothing that would give me greater pleasure, Lady de Vere."

The End

Home For Christmas

Cheryl Bolen

Copyright © 2012 by Cheryl Bolen

Home For Christmas is a work of fiction. Names, characters, places, and incidents are the products of the author's imagination or are used fictitiously. Any resemblance to actual events, locales, or persons, living or dead, is entirely coincidental.

All rights reserved.

No part of this publication may be reproduced, stored or transmitted in any form or by any means without the prior written permission of the author.

Chapter 1

Only a mad man would be riding his horse along a remote country road on so bitterly cold a day. Captain David St. Vincent was not mad. His impatience to be home in Ramseyfield after a six-year absence accounted for the rash judgment that brought him so close to the village where he'd spent his youth. In defense of his sanity, it should be noted the skies were perfectly sunny, and the temperature had been mild when he had set off from Fulchester earlier that day.

His eagerness to behold his family in Ramseyfield—as well as a certain beauty who resided there—was more powerful than the misery from chilling winds and strengthening snowfall. Neither his greatcoat nor his leather gloves offered sufficient protection against the elements. The prospect of riding within an enclosed carriage held vast appeal, though Captain St. Vincent would never ask a coachman to expose himself to such foul weather on his behalf.

During his six years in the Royal Navy sailing the seas and fighting the bloody French, the captain had learned not to dwell on unpleasant experiences—like gales that pitched his frigate on its side or French sailors trying to take off his head with a cutlass. He had nearly mastered the art of replacing the horrifying with the sublime. At least in his mind.

And nothing was more sublime than Miss

Elizabeth Balfour. The memory of her fair blond beauty had sustained him during the years of his absence. Every day for the past six years he had lamented he'd not offered for her before he left. At the time, he had expected to be home in a year, two at the most. During that time, she would reach a more acceptable marriageable age.

No one had then known how that Corsican monster would trample an entire continent. Thank God the fiend was now on Elba.

As welcome as his mother's letters had been, nothing had been more welcome than her observation about Miss Balfour still being unmarried. He would tell himself she had not found anyone who could supplant him in her heart. By her previous actions toward him, he believed she favored him over all the other young men who made cakes of themselves over her.

He could still recall the last time he saw Miss Balfour as if it were the past week. It had been May Day, and the sixteen-year-old Miss Balfour had been twirling around the maypole in the village green, her saffron skirts swirling, her silvery-blond locks whipping into that flawless face with its wide eyes as clear a blue as an Alpine lake. Every male in the shire was there that day, and not a one was immune to her abundant charms.

Now, as Captain St. Vincent's face stung and his ears throbbed from the miserable cold, he could picture Miss Balfour's lovely smile and her perfect white teeth, and he could almost hear the sweet trill of her voice. These memories nearly made him forget his discomfort.

He smelt a wood fire and looked up to see its source. The Mintons' cottage was just ahead. As he rode past the wattle-and-daub thatched cottage with smoke spiraling from its chimney, a deep sense of wellbeing spread over him like his grandmother's counterpane.

He was almost home.

He hoped he could get to Rosemary Hill, his family's big comforting farmhouse, before it became completely dark. It seemed as if the skies were blackening as quickly as an artist's brush could spread jet paint.

A kick to the flank spurred his mount to a faster clip.

Ten minutes of hard and fast riding later, he thought he saw a lone woman walking alongside the road. Surely it could not be! Not in this weather. And not so far away from any houses. Were her cloak not of a light color, he might never have seen her against the darkening skies.

As he drew nearer, he saw that she pressed her cloak's dove gray hood to her head so the assaulting winds would not blow it off. The slender female sped down the lane, her step youthful, her boots leaving indentations in the fresh snow. The wind behind them sounded like the forlorn howl of an injured animal.

She must be mad.

Mad or not, she was a helpless female, and he was a gentleman who intended to offer her assistance. He had to get her into a warm place before she froze to death. But what manner of lady would climb upon the horse of a stranger and ride off with him?

There was nothing for it. He must insist on trading places with her. Surely his sturdy boots were better suited to traipse across snow than were a lady's thin-soled ones. There was also the consideration that as a man, he was much more physically capable of coping with nature's brutality than a frail female.

His horse pulled up beside her. He knew he must shout to be heard over that dashed wind. "I say, miss!"

Her hand still pressing the wind-ruffled hood to her head, her gaze spun to him, and a smile instantly replaced the quizzing look that had been on her face.

She was even younger than he'd at first thought. Not having been in the company of English ladies of good birth for many years, he was not confident he could determine her age with any accuracy, but he was certain she could not exceeded twenty—which would make her seven years younger than he.

At first glance, the sight of her had sent his stomach flipping like a fish in its net. For a fleeting second he thought this girl was the incomparable Miss Balfour, but his lingering gaze told him this young lady lacked Miss Balfour's considerable beauty.

Had he been so long removed from decent females that he would think every blond lady bore a resemblance to his Incomparable?

"Why, if it isn't David St. Vincent! Welcome home."

Uh oh. The lady remembered him. But he did not remember her. How should he respond? He mustn't injure her feelings by admitting he had no memory of the lady. "It's glad I am to be home, and it appears I'm just in time to rescue a maiden in distress. I beg that you climb up here and allow me to take you home." Once he knew where she lived, he would know who she was.

Thank God he wouldn't have to trade places with her. Owing to their previous acquaintance—even if he had no recollection of it—she should have no aversion to sharing his mount. He dismounted in order to assist her in mounting.

She favored him with a wondrous smile. Perhaps she was pretty, after all, even though she was not the great beauty Miss Balfour was. He saw now that the hair beneath her hood was almost the same silken blond as Miss Balfour's. "Oh, David, you're my knight in shining armor!"

David? What lady would call him by so intimate a name? Only one who knew him well would do so, one who knew him very well. Which made him feel bloody stupid.

"You mustn't think me an empty-headed female who gets lost in blizzards. I assure you I'm normally an excessively prudent . . . woman. I never would have left Stoneyway had I any inkling the weather would change so dramatically."

Stoneyway! Why, that was the name of the house where Miss Elizabeth Balfour resided. Which would make this. . . this girl/woman her younger sister, Catherine. He never would have taken her for Cathy. The last time he'd clamped eyes on her, she was a bitty thing. "Cathy! I can't believe it! You're all grown up. Why, I still think of you as . . ." He leveled his hand out to show a height somewhere between his waist and his shoulders. "You couldn't have been more than twelve the last time I saw you."

"I was twelve and a half. I'm nineteen now." Pride gave stridency to her voice.

His brows elevated. "I trust your last name remains unchanged."

She nodded.

"Do you remember what you called me when you were a wee little girl?"

"Of course I do, but surely you're not going to embarrass me by bringing it up."

"There's nothing to be embarrassed over. I thought it was delightful when you called me Dabid."

She giggled.

He gave her a leg up, handed her the reins, then he hopped up and swung his leg over the beast to mount behind her. His arms coming around her, he took control once again. "Do you remember what you told me before I left?"

She stiffened. "Pray, Mr. St. Vincent, I beg that you not embarrass me by referring to that!"

He chuckled. "Then I won't refer to it."

Obviously, the very mention of the topic embarrassed her into silence. After a few minutes of clopping along over the fresh snow, he spoke. "Now, my dear young lady, you must tell me what lunacy brought you out on a day like this. I daresay this involves an unfortunate dog or cat."

She shook her head, almost dislodging the gray hood. "No dogs or cats. Since Mama died, I've moved up from aiding unfortunate animals to aiding unfortunate widows and children and the elderly."

He remembered the kindly Mrs. Balfour always coming to the aid of the needy in her husband's flock. His mother's letters had informed him of Mrs. Balfour's death three years previously. "I am so sorry for your loss. Your mother was one of the finest women it's ever been my honor to know."

She lowered her head and spoke in a barely audible voice. "Thank you."

"It's good that you're carrying on your mother's

benevolent ways. Pray, Cath, who were you aiding today?"

She shook her head. "You wouldn't know her. She's from down in Sussex. Fredrick Williamson met her when he was visiting with his sister. They fell in love, married, and he brought her back to Ramseyfield." Her voice lowered. "She's Frederick's widow now."

He winced. "Poor Frederick. I hadn't heard."

"You wouldn't have. He died just weeks ago."

"In the mines?"

She nodded ruefully. "His poor wife is prostrate—and her babe is due any day. I cannot tell you how my heart goes out to her."

"In what way were you able to help her?"

"I took her some fresh cheese, and I like to look in on her each day since she's so alone now. It would be terrible if the babe came and no one was there to help her."

"She's very fortunate, then, to have you."

They rode on in silence for a few moments before he spoke again. "I expect your sister's of great assistance in such matters of charity."

"Elizabeth's exceedingly tender hearted, so much so that it's difficult for her to observe the less fortunate. She prefers to turn her attention to happier matters. At present, there's no room in her head for anything save preparations for an assembly on Christmas Eve."

"I recall how much she liked to dance."

"Who wouldn't—when every male in the shire is queuing up to dance with one?"

"So she's still as beautiful as ever?"

"Indeed she is."

"I will own, I was surprised to learn from my mother's letters that Miss Balfour remains unmarried."

The younger sister shrugged. "It is not because she hasn't had ample opportunity to marry."

"Then she's rejected many offers?"

"Many."

Just as he would have thought. "Is there a particular reason why she has avoided matrimony?" Dare he hope she was waiting for his return?

"Particular is the key word, my dear Mr. St. Vincent."

So now she addressed him in the manner Society demanded. A pity. He liked it better when she'd called him by his Christian name.

Cathy shrugged. "I daresay someone as lovely as Elizabeth might aspire to something. . . more than can be found in Ramseyfield. There is the fact my aunt—you will remember my father's sister, Kate?—keeps putting ridiculous ideas into Elizabeth's pretty head, keeps telling her that one as beautiful as she could aspire to marry at least a baronet—or possibly higher."

His heart sank. Would marriage to a mere captain in his majesty's Royal Navy not suffice?

It had never occurred to him that he could be rejected now that he was in possession of an income many times greater than he'd ever thought to possess. When David had left Ramseyfield, he'd been a younger son with no financial prospects. Now, six years later, he could afford to buy his own farm. He'd even thought he might be able to afford one with a substantial house, larger than that which had been passed down in the St. Vincent family for the past two hundred years.

It had never crossed his mind that the lovely

Elizabeth Balfour would hunger for a title. He did a quick mental survey of Ramseyfield and the surrounding villages in an attempt to identify the men who bore titles.

Fortunately, Ramseyfield was void of titled gentlemen. Over in Swinford, there was Sir Reginald Boddley, but he was many years older than Miss Balfour and quite happily wed.

David's mind raced over the surrounding villages. Ah! Belford Manor in Ashton Mill was owned by the Earl of Haworth, but since Belford was one of his smaller properties, the wealthy peer had never visited there during David's entire childhood. That didn't mean an heir of his—perhaps a bachelor heir—wouldn't take a fancy to Belford and make his home there. Who wouldn't want to live here? In David's opinion, the Cumbria landscape was the loveliest in all of England.

The last titled person who came to mind was Lord Doncaster, who resided in Leffington some ten miles away. That baron had to be getting along in years. He could be dead for all David knew. David's pulse accelerated. What if Lord Doncaster were succeeded by a handsome *younger* man? Just because Lord Doncaster had not sired any sons did not mean his heir couldn't be a young, handsome bachelor. David hoped to God that was not the case. He swallowed. "Does Miss Balfour even know a baronet?"

Cathy giggled. "No, she doesn't. Papa and I try most sincerely to push such silly ideas from my sister's beautiful head."

Mr. Balfour was a very wise man. His Sunday sermons always demonstrated a remarkable degree of intelligence. The vicar's maiden sister, though, was quite another thing. David's mother had little patience with the foolish woman. Mrs. St. Vincent, a woman in possession of a considerable degree of intelligence, frequently remarked that Kate Balfour was in want of good sense.

He now had verification of his mother's opinions. Imagine, filling pretty Miss Balfour's head with notions of marrying a title!

Straight ahead he saw the lighted windows of Stoneyway. How good it felt to be back in Ramseyfield! His heart swelled, filling him with such a deep sense of appreciation, it was almost palpable.

Eyeing the Balfour home, he thought of all those previous times he'd been there as a child and as a young man. He never knew then what a privilege it was to live here in Ramseyfield. It had taken hundreds of lonely nights in strange, often hostile lands for him to understand the welcoming comfort of the place where he'd been born, the deep affection he felt for the people he'd known over the course of a lifetime.

He was aware that when he beheld his own house and his own much-beloved mother and siblings, his reaction would be even more profound.

Though he longed to see Miss Elizabeth Balfour, he knew that even a quick visit could rob him of still-passable roads. If he waited much later, it would be impossible to get home to his family tonight.

"I do hope, Mr. St. Vincent, you are home for good now. How often we have thought of you and prayed that you'd return safely."

"I must be getting quite old for all I've been able to think of is settling down in Ramseyfield with my own farm."

"I suppose as the captain of a vessel you've scooped in your share of bounty."

He nodded. "I've been fortunate."

"That's wonderful! Did you know Lord Haworth has decided to sell Belford Manor?"

"What, Miss Balfour, are you suggesting?" Even the hint that he could take up residence in that stately old pile set his pulse racing.

"I was hoping—for your sake—that you could afford to consider purchasing it."

Surely if he were in possession of Belford Manor the beautiful Miss Elizabeth Balfour would be most agreeable to uniting her life with his. "I don't know if my pockets are that deep."

"I heard that since Lord Haworth has not taken especially good care of it in recent years—owing to his deplorable addiction to faro—he may let it go cheaply."

He found himself confusing Cathy's more mature voice with her sister's, and the two now seemed indistinguishable. But, of course, he hadn't heard Elizabeth speak in years.

It wasn't just their voices which seemed to blend. Unless Elizabeth had grown considerably, he thought the two sisters were built remarkably alike. Both were of medium height, which was considerably shorter than he. And both were on the slender side but he remembered Elizabeth being pleasingly rounded in the places where a woman should be rounded.

He could almost believe it was Elizabeth's back brushing against his chest, almost believe that sweet rose scent were Elizabeth's, and only with the greatest restraint was he able to resist encircling the younger Miss Balfour with arms that ached to hold her sister. "Then be assured that as soon as the snow abates, I shall make inquiries about Belford Manor."

"It's so wonderful having you home again." Her head spun as if she were trying to see his face behind her. "Is this to be a surprise for your mother, or does she know you're coming?"

He turned onto the lane to Stoneyway. "A little bit of both, actually. I told her in my last letter I'd be home for Christmas, but she doesn't know when I'm to arrive."

"How I wish I could see the dear woman's face when she beholds you after so long!"

Cathy had always been a great favorite of his mother. And of everybody, actually. "By the way," he said, "I have something to return to you. A Balfour Family heirloom. Do you even remember giving it to me?"

"Of course I remember! I knew Grandpapa's cross would keep you safe." Now she did turn enough that he could see her profile outlined against the smoke-colored skies. "I was so afraid I- - -we'd never see you again."

His voice softened. His free hand settled gently at her slim waist. "I've never taken it off these past six years."

As they came to a stop not twenty feet from her front door, his emotions were conflicted. On the one hand he hated to terminate this conversation with Cathy. He was disappointed, too, that he would not be able to feast on the vision of Elizabeth. But he was equally as impatient to be at his own home, to be with his own family after so long an absence. Each moment of delay would make it more difficult to get home over roads that were obliterated by snow.

It was as if she could read his thoughts. "I don't suppose you can come in tonight?"

He shook his head as he dismounted. "I must make haste before the snows fall even harder." He helped her down.

She offered her hand. "Promise you will call on us the minute the roads clear."

He brushed his lips across the back of her hand and bowed. "I give you my word."

Elizabeth flung her arms around Cathy's neck before her sister could even remove her wet cloak. "I was beyond miserable with worry over you! I feared we'd find your corpse frozen to death. How could you put us into such a fright?"

Cathy shook the snow from her cloak and hung it on a wall peg. "It was a perfectly fair day when I left at noon."

Elizabeth's brows lowered. "Did I hear the sound of a horse bringing you home?"

"Indeed you did. You will never guess who rescued me from my icy misery." Stripping off her gloves, Cathy went straight to the hearth to warm her icy fingers.

"Then I beg that you just tell me."

Cathy almost hated to. For those few minutes she had liked to think she had David all to herself. He was perhaps the only thing on earth she did not want to share with her sister.

She'd been so happy with the dark knight who'd rescued her from the frozen path.

How she treasured their solitary ride that frigid evening. How she treasured everything about the most handsome man in the entire Royal Navy.

She knew, though, that once David and Elizabeth saw one another, she would never spend a single minute alone with him again.

He had never told Cathy he was in love with her sister, but she had often observed the way he hungrily looked at Elizabeth. He would never look at the younger sister in a similar way. No matter how badly she wanted him to.

"Actually it was David St. Vincent. Captain St. Vincent."

Her overly dramatic sister clutched at her chest, her mouth gaping open. "David's home?" Her eyes sparkled like crushed crystal. "You must tell me, is he as handsome as ever?"

Cathy pictured him as he'd stood there in the snow, tall and exceedingly handsome as his hands clasped her waist to hoist her atop the horse. His greatcoat had stretched over broad shoulders, his dark hair spilled onto his fine, masculine face. Her heartbeat drummed at the memory of the man. And she nodded.

"Why did you not ask him in?" Elizabeth pouted, something she did frequently and to great effect.

"Had he dallied even for a minute, he might not have been able to reach home. The snow seemed to get heavier with each passing minute."

Elizabeth shrugged. "He could have stayed in Papa's room." Her lower lip puckered into a perfect pout.

Cathy glared at her sister. "Honestly, Elizabeth, consider the poor man's feelings! He hasn't seen his family in six long years."

"There is that, I suppose." Her pout stayed.

As dearly as she loved her sister, Cathy did not feel like talking to her right now. In fact, she merely wanted to go to her bedchamber. And remember every torturing word, touch, or glance that had passed between her and the man she had always loved.

For her love of David St. Vincent was the only secret she had ever kept from her sister.

Chapter 2

Miss Catherine Balfour's head was filled with just one thing: a very handsome officer, though she'd sooner forfeit her well-loved and completely spoiled Fluffs than admit to her obsession over David St. Vincent. In all other respects, she was competent, pragmatic, and relatively intelligent. Except in matters pertaining to a certain recently returned captain in the Royal Navy.

She may have refrained from giving voice to her thoughts of him, but those thoughts had done a thorough job the past three days of robbing her of rational judgment.

There had lamentably been the incident where she absently locked Fluffs in her linen press and sat down to read Scott while petting the shawl folded in her lap—completely oblivious to her poor cat's screeches.

And she still had not come up with a plausible story to explain how she could have mistaken the post boy for her youngest brother. He was a full head shorter than Matthew and of swarthy complexion. All of the Balfours were very blond.

She had even provided entertainment at the dinner table the previous night by pouring beef gravy into one of Mama's lovely stemmed crystal glass. "I declare," Aunt Kate had chastised, her eyes wide with surprise, "I have never seen my level-headed niece act so scatter brained."

"I will own," Matthew responded, "Cathy's

acting more like Elizabeth."

Except for the similarity in their hair color, Cathy had never been compared to her elder sister—unless it be by someone uncharitably questioning how so beautiful a girl could have so plain a sister.

In the three days since she had seen David, Cathy had developed an inordinate curiosity about the weather. It was a wonder she had not worn thin the Turkey carpet between her desk chair and the window from her incessant trips to peer at the bleak winter landscape. She knew he would come once the snow cleared, and not an hour passed that she did not observe the relentless snowfall, willing it to go away.

On the fourth morning, she had awakened to radiant skies even though a great chill still hung in the air. *David will come today*, she had told herself as she dressed in her warmest garments in order to visit poor Mrs. Williamson and return in time for David's afternoon call. It always puzzled her that *morning* calls were paid in the afternoon.

That afternoon, she was returning to Stoneyway later than she would have liked, but she had not wanted to leave the unfortunate widow until she was better able to raise her spirits. When Cathy had arrived at the dark little Williamson cottage, the poor widow had not even attempted to draw open the curtains to allow in the day's meager light.

She had sat in front of the fire in the dark little room, knitting for her babe. "Oh, Miss Balfour, it is so very good of you to come. Your visits are the only thing I have to look forward to."

"Now that simply isn't true, Mrs. Williamson.

You've got the babe—your very own flesh and blood—to look forward to."

The widow nodded. "I do look forward to having someone to love, someone who will love me as me Frederick did."

"You must remember how blessed you were to be loved by Frederick. Conceive that some women will go to their graves and never know a love like that." *Will I be one of those women? Like sour Aunt Kate.*

Though Mrs. Williamson was five years her senior, when she smiled up at Cathy, there was a child-like quality about her. "It always cheers me when you come, Miss Balfour. You bring cheer wherever you go."

"That makes me very happy to hear." Cathy handed her a wrapped piece of plum pudding. "Here, I know how much you like this."

"You are so thoughtful and kind." She quickly unwrapped it and broke off a piece to eat. "I hate to burden you with my problems, but you're the only person I have." Mrs. Williamson's eyes misted. "I dreamt last night that the babe was born dead."

How cruel it would be for the woman to suffer two such losses so close together! "I'm sorry you had such a wretched dream, but you must realize that's all it was: a dream. As long as your spirits stay so low, those melancholy thoughts will invade your dreams. I must encourage you each night before you go to bed to force yourself to think pleasant thoughts."

Cathy hated to leave Mrs. Williamson before she could brighten her outlook. When she finally felt comfortable enough to leave, she stood. "It's just four days until Christmas. I will save a place for you in our pew on Christmas morning."

"I hope my babe comes before Christmas."

Cathy shrugged. "It could be a Christmas baby."

"What a blessed Christmas gift that would be!"

By the time Cathy returned to Stoneyway, the St. Vincents' carriage was already there. Her spirits fell. She would not have the opportunity to change into a more feminine or more flattering dress. She would have to greet the man of her dreams in her serviceable woolen frock while her beautiful sister would no doubt be stunning in something delicate and utterly lovely. Why should it matter what she wore? No man would ever even look at her as long as Elizabeth was in the same chamber.

As she moved along the lane, she remembered David reminding her of the last words she'd said to him when she was twelve and a half and had no sense of delicacy. It still embarrassed her that he knew her secret when not even her own sister suspected. How grateful she was that he had the decency not to repeat those embarrassing words when they had met again!

Inside her house, she was still shaking her head at her foolishness six years previously. How could she have been so humiliatingly honest? Obviously, she had been completely devoid of pride. She'd had six years in which to restore that pride, and she vowed to never again humiliate herself in such a way.

David's deep chuckle came from the drawing room. She removed her cloak, pelisse, and gloves before taking a deep breath and strolling into the drawing room.

David and his elder brother Michael rose when

she entered. She politely greeted them as well as Michael's pretty wife, Georgianne, before taking her place on the faded green brocade sofa next to her sister.

How natural it looked to see David sitting there in the high-backed upholstered armchair. How happy it made her to have him here in her favorite room. This chamber, more than any at Stoneyway, bore Mama's stamp. She had brought the pianoforte—and many other lovely things—when she married Papa. The painting over the hearth was of Mama's grandmother. Cathy's gaze flicked to the striped silk draperies which had been pulled away from each of the tall windows. Their silk complemented the green silk brocade Mama had selected when she'd come to Stoneyway as a bride. As a newlywed, Mama had sewn them herself.

"Please, my dear Miss Balfour," David said to her, "tell me you did not walk all the way to the Williamson cottage in this cold!"

Her eyes flashed with mirth. "Then I won't tell you."

Elizabeth beamed at David. "My sister has a most stout constitution—and she adores walking—which allows her to carry on with the family's benevolent works."

"Poor Miss Elizabeth," their Aunt Kate added, "is not possessed of such robust health. I positively must put my foot down and not allow her to go traipsing about the countryside—no matter how much her tender heart calls on her to minister to the poor of the parish."

Brows lowered, Cathy spun to Elizabeth. "I have never thought of you as not having robust health, and I've spent every day of my life in your presence! Is there some terrible malady you're hiding from me?"

"If you will think back to last winter, you will recall that horrid cough that sent me to bed."

Cathy nodded. "Of course I recall it. I was already in bed with fever!"

"I am quite convinced had I not gone to bed I, too, would have come down with a fever."

"Elizabeth's so delicate," Kate said to the visitors.

David's gaze flicked from aunt to settle appreciatively on delicate niece.

A moment later, he turned his attention once more to Cathy. "How was Mrs. Williamson? Has the baby come?"

Cathy was disappointed that he—and not her sister and aunt who were actually acquainted with the unfortunate widow—was the one to inquire about her. She shrugged. "She's very low. The babe has still not come, and she grows more melancholy as Christmas nears. Had we another bed, I would have brought her home with me. How can the poor woman even send for the midwife when she's so alone?"

"Now, dearest," Aunt Kate said, "you can't bring all the unfortunate souls in the parish to live under our roof. My brother will be the first to tell you so."

"I know, it's just so heart wrenching."

David's gaze cut once more to her. "I remember well how Miss Catherine was always trying to bring home what she called orphaned dogs and cats."

"We must speak no more of sad topics," Elizabeth said. "The captain has the most splendid news! He's going to look at Belford

Manor this afternoon. He may purchase it from Lord Haworth." Elizabeth could neither disguise her affection for David nor her enthusiasm over the potential purchase of Belford. It had been a long time since she had been impressed over a gentleman caller. "Dare we ask if we could come while you look at it?" Elizabeth peered at him through lowered lashes.

"You girls can go on without me," Aunt Kate said, looking across the Oriental carpet at the visitors, "that is, if there's room in your carriage for my nieces."

Michael St. Vincent, who sat next to his wife on a silk damask settee, hugged her. "I can always put Georgie on my lap."

Aunt Kate's eyes narrowed. She had never approved of public displays of affection.

Cathy turned to her sister. "You must change into warmer clothing. It's beastly cold out there." Elizabeth wore a spring-like dress of sprigged muslin which completely exposed her arms and displayed the tops of breasts straining beneath the scooped bodice. She looked incredibly delicate.

Elizabeth pouted. "I suppose I must." Her disdainful glance fell on Cathy's ugly brown wool dress.

"That is," Cathy added, turning her gaze to David, "if we shall be permitted on this journey. You have every right to want to purvey so important a purchase without two babbling females in tow, meaning, of course, my sister and me."

"I would be delighted to have the sisters Balfour accompany me. I should value a female's opinion."

"Then my sister and I shall be honored to be included in your party," Elizabeth said.

While Elizabeth went upstairs to don warm clothing, Cathy said, "I must apologize that Papa has not come to greet you. He buries himself in the library each day. Had he known you'd come home, I daresay he'd have flown out of the musty chamber." She stood. "Pray, Captain, let us go and see Papa."

Aunt Kate's brows lowered. "You know your father does not like to be interrupted when he's in his library."

"My dear aunt, I assure you Papa would be angry not to be informed that David St. Vincent is at long last home. David's a great favorite with Papa." *Uh oh.* She had slipped and called him David. Hopefully none of the others noticed.

"Are you certain I won't be imposing on your father?" David asked as he stood.

"I am absolutely certain."

Papa's library was just across the hall. "Look, Papa, who's come home."

If the drawing room bore her mother's stamp, the library bespoke Mr. Balfour's introspective personality almost as thoroughly as a portrait bespoke his physical appearance. Every shelf was crammed with a vast assortment of books on every topic. Some had been purchased new, most second hand, and a few were gifts from young men he had tutored in the classics over the years. The wall of shelves was not enough to hold all the clergyman's books. They stacked in teetering columns on the floor, with many other book stacks surrounding his desk.

He sat at his desk, which was piled high with stacks of papers. Its drawers were so crammed with old letters, they could not be closed but reposed at varying degrees of openness.

The moment he beheld David, a smile brightened his craggy face, and he leapt to his feet. "David St. Vincent! You are home! What a happy day this is!"

Cathy beamed. David was almost as special to her father as he was to her.

While he had fully intended to finagle a seat in the coach next to the Incomparable, somehow she ended up sitting across the carriage from him. True to his jovial word, Michael had yanked Georgianne onto his lap, and the disgustingly happy husband and wife were seated beside the beauty. As he settled back into the squabs, David realized this seating arrangement worked very well since it afforded him the opportunity to openly gaze upon the extraordinary Miss Elizabeth Balfour.

The wistful memories of her fair blond loveliness that had invaded his daydreams and night dreams for years had not embellished her beauty at all. As a woman of two and twenty, she had grown even more beautiful than she had been when he last saw her at sixteen. How stupendously fortunate he was that she had not married.

That lady bestowed a bright smile upon him. "I am so happy you are home, Captain. You must come to our Christmas Eve assembly."

"To be fortunate enough to dance with you, Miss Balfour, I would tread through snow."

Her lashes lowered coyly.

Then he remembered his manners and turned to the plainer sister who sat beside him. "And I pray that you will also do me the goodness of standing up with me at the assembly, Miss Balfour."

Cathy favored him with a smile. "I would be honored." Even though the bracken color of her eyes was not as pretty or as striking as her sister's blue, there was something in the way they sparkled with such warmth that captivated him. He found himself staring at her before he quickly looked away.

"I am so excited about the assembly," Elizabeth said. "I am making a new dress just for it."

"What color?" Georgianne asked.

"Golden. And I'm embroidering its border with gold thread."

"How lovely!" Georgianne eyed Cathy. "And what color is yours?"

"It is the same green one I've worn to the last three assemblies." She shrugged. "I'm the practical sister."

"Enough talk of fashions!" Michael said. "I'd rather boast on my brother. He's quite the naval hero, you know?"

Miss Elizabeth Balfour's mouth gaped open. "I did not know!"

Miss Catherine Balfour turned to him. "My sister finds reading about sea battles utterly boring, but I read the accounts of every single battle during the war, and I saved any newspaper which mentioned you or one of your ships."

As surprised as he was that his actions had been reported in newspapers back in his homeland, David was equally surprised at Cathy's loyalty to him. His mouth curved into a smile as he remembered her as she looked when he'd left that day in his midshipman's uniform, how she had exclaimed, "I shall wait for you to come home and marry me for no one but you will ever do."

He had forgotten her proclamation until the other afternoon when he'd felt her back pressed against him as they shared his horse, his arms bracketing her. He had been shocked to realize that Cath was no longer that little girl who'd once called him Dabid. She was a woman now, and he was flooded with memories of that long-ago day.

Now in his brother's carriage, with the side of her leg pressing his, he was swamped again with awareness that little Cathy Balfour was now a grown woman.

He turned to her. "I am humbled, but not humbled enough that I wouldn't derive great pleasure from seeing those newspapers."

"I would be happy to show them to you."

He addressed his brother. "It is my good fortune to have had a loving family—as well Miss Catherine Balfour—praying for my safe return."

"La!" Elizabeth exclaimed. "I'm sure I, too, prayed for you."

As much as he wanted to believe this incredible creature had spared a thought for him during the years he was gone, somehow her words lacked sincerity. "I thank you, Miss Balfour."

"It was terrible the way Johnny Oliphant came home from the war!" Elizabeth scrunched up her nose in distaste. "If it wasn't bad enough that he lost his leg, he lost an eye, too. Poor thing. He was so handsome before." She shook her head. "Now I don't suppose any woman would have him."

Her words turned his stomach.

"That's a terrible thing to say," Cathy chided. "Johnny's still the kindly person he was before the war, though God knows he's endured enough to have changed him. And he gets around almost as well as a man with two good legs."

"Indeed he does," Michael added.

Elizabeth's brows lowered. "But the disfigurement!"

"Dearest," Cathy said, eying her sister, "I pray that just because you had the good fortune to be born beautiful doesn't mean that you put great stock in appearances."

Her lashes lowering in that unique way she had, Elizabeth tossed a quick glance at him. "I am sure I'm not that great a beauty! My nose could certainly be a bit straighter, and I do wish my hair would curl naturally." She shrugged. "It would make life so much easier."

Had she completely missed her sister's point? It was becoming abundantly clear to him that in the Balfour family the younger of the sisters had inherited their father's uncommon good sense while the elder possessed the mother's beauty—tenfold. To his utter disappointment, he had to admit The Beauty also seemed to have inherited her aunt's want of good sense.

Nevertheless, his heart still accelerated when he beheld her.

Since his return, he'd once again sensed that connection that had been between them before he left. As an adolescent lad, he had known by her flirty actions toward him Elizabeth favored him over all the others. Even then, she'd been proficient at lowering those eyelashes seductively and at favoring him with sultry gazes that caused his breath to grow short. Which it still did.

"Oh, dearest," Georgianne said to her husband, "don't forget we must invite the girls to dine with us tomorrow."

"Oh, yes. My friend from Oxford, Lord Neely, will be stopping by for a few days. The poor fellow has been orphaned, and being an only child, he has no family to visit at Christmas. Several of us that ran together at university have asked him to come spend Christmas with us, but it was I who was so singularly honored."

Georgianne smiled. "Because Lord Neely lives for shooting, and the shooting in Ramseyfield is very good."

"How delightful!" Elizabeth said. "Is. . . his lordship bringing his wife?"

Michael shrugged. "He has no wife, either. No family whatsoever."

Elizabeth smiled at her sister. "What great fun it will be to meet Lord Neely."

The sense of wellbeing that had buoyed him since his return vanished like the snuff of a candle. Yesterday he'd been fairly confident he would not have to compete with an aristocrat for the lady's hand.

And now he realized there would be no smooth sailing to marriage with the girl of his dreams. Why did that bloody viscount have to come before David secured Miss Elizabeth Balfour's hand in marriage? The viscount was sure to fall in love with so beautiful a maiden.

The very thought of Lord Neely put David in a foul mood.

When they arrived at Belford Manor, he was pleased that Elizabeth stood beside the carriage until he stepped out, then she possessively settled a hand upon his arm. Together, they led the way along the stone path to Belford's neoclassical portico.

He'd been told that staff no longer resided there, but the caretaker would see to it that the door was unlocked. As he stood there looking up at the substantial stone blocks of which the house was constructed, he was completely awed. He had never dreamed that the second son of gentleman farmer could ever afford such a residence.

By comparison to other country houses of the nobility, Belford was small. More like a dowager house. It had never been a seat but had come to the present earl through his grandmother, who had been the daughter of a duke. When David's mother was a girl, she had been a guest here and loved to reminisce about the fetes Lady Eleanor had held there. How happy his widowed mother would be to have her own chamber here.

He drew in a breath and entered this home he'd always admired but had never visited. At first it was difficult to see because the entry hall and all the rooms fanning out from it were so dark. Dust coated the floors, the window sills, and the furnishings. Several posts were missing from the stair's banister. There was a gaping circle in the ceiling where a chandelier had formerly suspended. The dated furnishings would stay with the house, but huge squares on the dirty walls showed where paintings had once hung.

In spite of all these things, the house was magnificent!

"Observe how tall the ceilings are!" Elizabeth exclaimed, her blue eyes dancing as she peered up more than thirty feet.

The pragmatic younger sister had set about opening draperies. "The chambers will be ever so much more delightful once we let in the light."

A smile on her pretty face, Elizabeth quickly led him to the first chamber on the left, a drawing room furnished with worn Turkey carpets and faded silks on the sofas and in the draperies. The ceiling here was not thirty feet, but it was considerably taller than those in the St. Vincent home, which was one of the more vastly admired houses in the shire.

A stranger seeing him and Elizabeth race from one room to the other would surely have taken them either for a married couple or one that was betrothed for Elizabeth had adopted a most proprietary air toward him. He thought such actions would have intoxicated him more than they did.

Once the five of them had viewed every room—with Cathy running ahead and throwing draperies open to enhance their experience—they came back to the morning room.

Elizabeth was as excited as she had been on that long-ago May Day when she'd twirled around the maypole. Even more so. "I know the very chamber which will be your ballroom!"

Ballroom? He had been far more interested in the master and mistress's chambers. And the nursery. "I hadn't thought of balls."

"I believe the captain is looking to settle down," Cathy said.

Elizabeth's mouth gaped open. "Have you. . . an understanding with a particular lady?"

That she looked so apprehensive boosted his pride. His gaze met hers. "No particular lady."

Their eyes caught and held. The Beauty was clearly conveying her interest. He looked away.

"Tell me this," Elizabeth said, demanding his attention return to her, "is what my sister said true? Are you wanting to settle down?"

His glance moved to Michael and Georgianne. "Since my brother so enthusiastically espouses the benefits of matrimony, I think it might suit me."

For some unaccountable reason, he turned to Cathy. "Do you think I should buy Belford Manor?"

She shrugged. "I cannot advise you or anyone on so grave a step. With a bit of care, Belford will be lovely home again, and if it's your desire to live here, I hope it will be in your power to gain ownership." It was the same type of comment her wise father would have made.

On the return journey, the seating arrangements were the same. He spoke little because his plans for Belford spun through his mind like a gristmill. The minute he had glimpsed the old structure rising proudly from the pastoral landscape, he knew he wanted it.

The sisters Balfour also occupied his mind. How could two sisters from the same two parents be so vastly different?

When they reached Stoneyway he asked Cathy if he could call on her the following morning to see the newspaper accounts she had saved. "And when I say morning, I mean morning. I know you ladies will be spending the afternoon beautifying yourselves for dinner with Lord Neely." He knew it, but he didn't like it.

"I would love to see the newspapers, too," Elizabeth said.

"My dearest," Cathy said, turning to her sister, "I'll show them to you straight away. I had no idea you'd be interested."

"I prefer to see them with the Captain so he

can give us a personal accounting. How exciting it will be to hear about his heroic exploits."

Again, he felt Elizabeth's words lacked sincerity.

On the way back to Rosemary Hill, David and his brother and sister-in-law discussed the merits and pitfalls of purchasing Belford Manor, then Michael turned the conversation back to the ladies they had just left at Stoneyway. "Miss Elizabeth Balfour seems to be taking an interest in all things to do with Captain David St. Vincent."

"She's an utterly lovely girl, David," Georgianne said.

"Indeed she is." David cleared his throat. "I will own that I have spent the last six years praying she would still be unmarried when I returned."

Georgianne's big brown eyes rounded. "Does that mean you're going to offer for her?"

"I may."

His brother cleared his throat. "Tomorrow night—should you prefer to have Miss Elizabeth seated next to you?"

Georgianne clearly had something to add. "Elizabeth Balfour's beauty would be a powerful bait to lure in a viscount."

"As much as I want to claim her affections—and as much as I fear I will not be able to compete with a viscount—I would not wish to marry a woman who found me second best."

"That is wise of you," Michael said. "I shall seat her next to Lord Neely."

"I think she will prefer David. He *is* more handsome than the viscount—for your brother looks very much like you, my love."

David shrugged. "If Elizabeth Balfour should

prefer Neely over me, then I pray he returns her ardor."

"Until today, I would have said she has been saving herself in the hopes of snaring a man of a higher station than is generally met with in Ramseyfield," Georgianne said.

David eyed her. "And today?"

"Today I believe she is smitten with you."

Chapter 3

Miss Elizabeth Balfour's beauty nearly stole his breath the following morning as she descended the stairs to greet him. Her whitish blond tresses swept away from that flawless face of hers, and her feminine spring-like dress displayed the slope of her breast and revealed milky shoulders that were only partially covered by a red shawl. "La, Captain! Can you conceive that I am dressed and ready to face callers at so early an hour?"

He took her hand, bowed, and greeted her. "Another lady with a month to prepare could never look as lovely as you, my dear Miss Balfour."

Almost as an afterthought he remembered the sister who had apparently read with great interest all things that pertained to his naval escapades. When he peered over Elizabeth's shoulder, he half expected to see Cathy as she'd looked at eleven when she gave him the cross he would return to her today.

But it was not an eleven-year-old who greeted him after her sister. It was a fully grown woman. A woman with a woman's breasts. Looking at the two sisters together, he realized they were the same height, the same slender weight, and had the same pale hair. Only one had a beautiful face; the other did not—not that Cathy's face was not a nice face.

He could not take Cathy's hand because she

carried a wide, flat box. "I thought that since there are three of us," she said, "we could all see the newspapers better if we gather at the dining table."

He and Elizabeth followed her to that chamber where a large walnut table centered the long room. More faded silk draperies hung here from a row of three tall casements. Cathy set the box at the midpoint between the head and foot of the table, then looked up at him. "Should you like to sit between us, so you can elaborate on the writings?"

"I can attempt to—even though I suspect you know more about what's in that box than I."

He pulled out a chair for each of the ladies before he took his seat.

It was then that their aunt entered the chamber to serve as chaperone. He rose quickly, bowed, and courteously greeted her.

The skinny old maid with silver streaking her mousy locks had brought along a sewing basket and a garment of some kind. "Pray, Captain, don't spare a thought for me. I'll just sit where the light is good and work on my sewing."

"Pray, let me know if you need assistance of any kind." He returned to his chair. "My mother often calls on me to thread her needles because her eyes are not as good as they once were."

Miss Kate Balfour laughed. "My nieces typically perform that function for me."

Seated, he removed the box's lid. "Are the newspapers in chronological order?" he asked Cathy.

"Yes. The first, you will see, dates from about five years ago. I knew from your brother that you were serving on the H.M.S. *Avalon*. So when I saw the *Avalon* mentioned here, I read it with great interest."

As he did now. The frigate *Avalon* was the smallest vessel he'd sailed upon during his naval career, but it had played an instrumental part in the successful British blockade against the French at Gibraltar. How remarkable that Cathy had saved this particular account since the actions that had occurred there significantly impacted his naval career.

"I got my first commission after that," he commented. The long-desired commission had not come without cost. Two of the *Avalon's* officers—both good men—had been killed in action there near Gibraltar.

His glance swept to a bowl of currants in the center of the table. He fetched a handful of them and began to line them up to illustrate the positions of both the French and British fleet and set about explaining what had to occur to block the French.

Miss Elizabeth Balfour's hands clutched at her chest. "I declare! You must have been in great danger."

"There is always danger when the enemy is that close."

Next, he continued to peruse the yellowed newspapers the thoughtful Miss Catherine Balfour had read with apparent interest and so carefully saved. From the frigate, he'd stepped up to a seventy-four gun man-of-war, the H.M.S. *Richmond*.

Despite that he'd often wanted to correspond with Miss Elizabeth Balfour, he was not permitted to write to an unmarried lady to whom he was not engaged. Or to her sister. His gaze whirled to

Cathy. "How was it possible for you to so closely monitor my naval career?"

"I'm afraid I made a pest of myself, badgering your brother for information every Sunday on the steps of church."

The wrong sister.

"I'm humbled by your interest."

"Now that you're home, it will be my pleasure to present you the box."

He was incredibly touched that she was now willing to give him the contents of this box she had spent years assembling. He was far too interested and far too appreciative to turn down her generous offer. Their eyes met. He felt tremendous affection for her. Of course, not the same kind of affection he'd held for her sister all these many years. The affection he held for Cathy was more like one would feel toward a younger sister. But altogether different.

"No gift has ever meant more to me," he murmured. He wanted to tell her another gift she had bestowed upon him had been as appreciated, but for reasons he could not understand, he did not want Elizabeth to know about the cross Cathy had pressed into his hand on that far-off day. It was a memory he liked to hold close in the same way that cross fitted to his chest and kept him safe these last several years.

"You must tell me, Captain," Elizabeth said, sliding a sideways glance at him while lowering her lengthy lashes most alluringly, "is it true that press gangs force innocent young men aboard his majesty's ships to serve as sailors?"

He hung his head. "It's a lamentable practice, but I will own that it's a wide-spread practice that's accepted because things have always been done in such a manner."

Cathy spoke almost reverently. "Lord Nelson agreed with you. I read where he said men should flock to the Royal Navy to proudly serve their country, not to serve because they were forced to do so."

"Ah, another matter upon which I agree with the late Lord Nelson," David said.

"I know Lord Nelson's been dead for an age now," Elizabeth said somberly. "Did you ever meet him?"

"I never met him, though I saw him once in Portsmouth. I was only sixteen or seventeen, and he was already famous because of the Battle of the Nile. Everywhere he went, he was hailed as a hero, and everyone stopped what they were doing to gawk at him. I confess I did, too."

"Pray, let us speak no more of Lord Nelson, or I shall grow melancholy," Elizabeth said.

"I am so grateful—as I am certain your family is—that you've returned safely, Captain." Everything that Cathy said and did was like a tender stroke to his psyche. How wonderful it was to be home again. And this time, for good.

He gathered up the sheets of newspaper, folded them, and restored them to the box. "I have many hours of interesting reading ahead of me whilst I enjoy these many accounts of my naval career."

"Have you given any more thought to purchasing Belford Manor?" Elizabeth asked.

He frowned. "It's a grave step. I slept little last night."

"I completely understand," Cathy said.

Elizabeth pouted. "You have not answered my question, Captain."

"That is because, Miss Elizabeth, I have not

made my decision yet."

He scooted his chair back and stood. "I am bereft of words to convey to you my deep appreciation," he said to Cathy as he removed the box from the table.

Both sisters rose. "You needn't say anything," Cathy told him. "Your interest in the box has repaid me tenfold."

"I shall leave you ladies now, but I look forward to having you dine with us tonight. My brother will send his carriage around to collect you at five. Will that be agreeable to you, Miss Balfour?" he asked Aunt Kate, who remained seated.

"Yes, my brother and I—and the girls—are excessively looking forward to it."

He wanted to have a private moment with Cathy without being conspicuous. They strolled from the room as Miss Kate Balfour called her eldest niece. He said goodbye to her, then asked Cathy to walk with him to the door.

When it was just the two of them facing each other, he set down the box. Then he fetched the cross from his pocket and held it out for her. "It seems I always find myself in your debt, my dear Miss Balfour." *My dear Miss Balfour* was so formal and stuffy a way to address his old friend. "I am unworthy of having a friend as loyal and considerate as you have been to me."

"I am happiest when serving those I care about."

"But you, my dear Miss Balfour, care about every one of God's creatures!"

A smile crossing her face, she nodded. "I cannot deny it."

Yet somehow he knew her feelings for him were special. And he was powerless not to recall that little girl telling him she would wait until his return because she meant to marry him.

A pity he was so unworthy of her affection.

It wasn't often a clergyman's daughter had the opportunity to ride in a fine carriage, and now she had enjoyed that privilege two days in a row—though it did not precisely look like a *day* at present, Cathy reflected as she peered from the coach's glass. Night fell early this time of year.

And with night had come a bitter cold.

She would have thought a carriage would provide more protection against the cold, but she and her sister, who sat next to her, shivered from the frigid temperatures. Being the pragmatic sister, Cathy had wisely donned her warmest clothing—at least for her outer garments, which were decidedly winterish. She had buttoned a green velvet pelisse over her rather skimpy frock, and a heavy wool hooded cloak layered over the pelisse. Her gloved hands were stuffed into a muff made from inexpensive rabbit fur.

Though she continued to wear the hood, her ears still stung from the cold. Her cheeks must be a deep red.

"Now don't you wish you had listened to me?" she said to her sister.

"I will own, you were right." Her teeth chattered so much it impeded her speech. "I should have worn a pelisse under my cloak, too. I am excessively cold. It's just that I wanted to project an elegant vision with my cloak lying over bare white shoulders."

"If you spent half the time reading Scripture as you do in front of your looking glass," their father grumbled, "you'd realize what things are truly important."

His comments silenced both daughters. A few minutes later, his grumbling continued. "Remind me again why it is that I'm having to leave the comfort of my home on such a night?"

"Because, my dear Papa," Elizabeth replied, "the St. Vincents have honored us with an invitation to dine with them and their guest, Lord Neely, at Rosemary Hill."

"Who is this Lord Neely?" Papa directed his question at Cathy. While Aunt Kate clearly preferred the beautiful daughter, Papa was closest to the more intelligent daughter.

"Lord Neely was friends with Michael St. Vincent when he was at Oxford," Elizabeth responded.

"Why would a titled gentleman be wanting to traipse about the country under such uncomfortably cold conditions?" Mr. Balfour continued to grumble. "Doesn't the fellow have his own seat?"

"I am sure he must," Elizabeth defended.

"I believe he's coming at this time of year to avoid being home alone," Cathy said. "The unfortunate man has no family with whom to spend Christmas."

Aunt Kate attempted to sooth her brother. "My dear brother, it's almost like Divine Providence is smiling upon our Elizabeth."

Mr. Balfour turned toward his sister, who sat next to him. "Have you attics to let? To what in God's wide, wide world can you be referring?"

"All these years I've encouraged Elizabeth to save herself for some titled gentleman who'd be worthy of her. And now she may be able to fulfill her destiny."

The vicar tossed his head back dismissively. "Pray, I wish you would not fill my daughter's head with such nonsense! All I've ever wanted for my children is for them to be as happy with their mates as I was with their dear mother."

Despite that she had unwisely balked at dressing appropriately for the weather, a shivering Elizabeth lifted her chin higher. "I think Aunt Kate is right, Papa. It *is* Divine Providence that Lord Neely is coming here this Christmas season."

"Then I lament it's Divine Providence that has saddled me with two such foolish maidens! I thank God Cathy, at least, has her wits about her."

The coach slowed, then came to a complete stop. Cathy glanced from the window at the large gray stone farm house, its slate roof blanketed with fresh snow. As they disembarked the carriage at the steps to the St. Vincents' big, comfortable house, Cathy silently questioned her sister's wits. How could someone be so vain that she would expose herself to such cold?

When they removed their outer garments in the entry hall, snowflakes puddle on the well-worn wooden floors. Cathy could not help but to observe the bluish cast to her sister's skin. "Really, dearest," she whispered hoarsely to Elizabeth, "you might wish to borrow a shawl from Mrs. St. Vincent."

"I am persuaded that if I just remove myself from this hall, I shall warm up."

The St. Vincent male servant led them into the drawing room which was warmed by a blazing fire in its hearth. Three gentlemen stood when they entered the chamber. Two of them were the St. Vincent brothers, and the third was a shorter man of the same age.

"Lord Neely," Michael St. Vincent said, "allow me to present to you our vicar, Mr. Balfour, who has come with his sister and his two daughters."

Cathy took the opportunity to observe the viscount. His light brown hair was stylishly cut, as were his clothes which consisted of a snowy white linen shirt and cravat beneath a fine black cutaway jacket, gray and red silk waistcoat, and gray superfine breeches. Though slight of build and height, he had a fine face with expressive green eyes and a friendly countenance, especially when Elizabeth placed her hand into his. "I cannot tell you how pleased I am that your Christian name is preceded by *Miss*," he told her in his lazy, aristocratic drawl.

Whisking her gaze over her sister, Cathy tried to look at her as would one who had never before seen her. How beautiful she looked! She wore a saffron-colored gown that fell off those milky white shoulders while affording a glimpse of her breasts' swell. She truly did appear elegant.

Even if she was tinged with blue.

The knowledge that David must be captivated over her sister's uncommon beauty could not instill jealousy in Catherine for she could never consider them rivals.

Elizabeth's lashes dipped in that coquettish manner of hers as Lord Neely continued to hold her hand. "My lord! You shall put me to the blush."

To Miss Catherine Balfour's knowledge, none of the volumes worth of praise bestowed upon her sister throughout her life had ever put Miss Elizabeth Balfour to the blush.

Perhaps Cathy's great interest in the

appearances of Elizabeth and Lord Neely was so she would not stare at David. She had never before seen him in his dashing captain's uniform, and she had never before seen him so handsome. Heavy gold braid and gold epaulets and shiny brass medals adorned his well-cut dark blue jacket. Could this distinguished officer be the David St. Vincent she had known throughout her life?

Her appreciative gaze raked over him as she were seeing him for the first time. Was it the sight of those long, powerful legs in white breeches that made her more aware than ever of his height?

She could almost picture him at the bow of a great man-of-war, commanding the hundreds of men who had sailed with him. Because of his kindliness, she had never before thought of him as powerful. Until tonight. Even the dark stubble on his face emanated a manliness that could demand the respect of an entire fleet.

Now Elizabeth would be sure to fall in love with him, too.

"I declare," Georgianne St. Vincent said, "now that everyone is here, we shall remove to the dining room."

A smile on his youthful-looking face, his lordship proffered his arm to their hostess and escorted her across the hall to the narrow dining room. Michael St. Vincent offered to escort Elizabeth, David courteously presented himself at Aunt Kate's side to escort her, and her father offered his crooked arm to David's mother, which left Cathy trailing the others like an extra shoe.

The dining chamber was being warmed by another roaring fire and was illuminated by wall sconces, the table's pair of ornate silver candelabra, and an overhead crystal chandelier. The seating arrangements were sure to satisfy both her and her sister. David was seated at Cathy's left while Elizabeth was seated across the table from David—and next to the viscount.

Watching her sister's flirty ways with the visiting aristocrat made Cathy feel rather like a student rapturously watching a master. Elizabeth's frequent inquiries to the man beside her would end with *What do you think, my lord?* She helplessly sought his assistance in cutting her roast beef. *I am so bereft of strength.* And Miss Elizabeth Balfour had elevated the lowering of her lashes to an art form. An art form that appeared to fascinate Lord Neely.

The only problem with the seating was that the beautiful sister was on blatant display for David to admire—even though he was wonderfully communicative with Cathy. "I must tell you again how much I appreciate all those newspaper accounts. I spent the afternoon reading every one of them."

"Had you read any of them before?"

He shook his head. "None."

"I would have thought your brother would have them."

"Oh, he did, but he confessed he never thought to save them for me. I'm very touched that you were so much more thoughtful, especially since you're not family. How can I ever repay you?"

"Your appreciation is my payment."

"Is there not some service I could perform for you? You are, after all, one of my dearest friends."

Not exactly what she wanted to hear. But close. "You must believe that what I did I did for my own pleasure—not that worrying over you was precisely pleasurable! But, since you have asked if there is a service you can perform me, I am not too proud to ask it."

His brows hiked. "Anything, my dear Miss Balfour."

She had liked it ever so much more when he used to call her Cathy. And sometimes just Cath. "I'm afraid what I'm going to ask for will be a great sacrifice for you. . ."

"I was not jesting. Anything."

Marry me? No, she could never ask that. Again. She was no longer twelve and a half years old. She cleared her throat. "If it weren't so bitterly cold, I would not ask, but you are aware that on a clergyman's living, the keeping of a carriage is beyond our family's means. Therefore, I shall beg that you borrow your brother's carriage to take me to look in on the unfortunate Mrs. Williamson—until her babe comes, and I expect it any day. I hate to ask. You must be looking forward to shooting with your brother and Lord Neely."

He shook his head. "Killing of any creature has no appeal—not for one who's seen as many violent deaths as I have."

To her astonishment, he looked upon her with great affection. "You are a remarkable young woman."

"You surely mistake me for someone else, Captain."

He shook his dark head. "No, Miss Balfour, it's you and only you who have made so strong an impression upon me."

Her eyes rounded. "Pray, how could I possibly make a strong impression on anyone?" Certainly not with her sadly lacking appearance. She was, after all, the mousy sister.

"I have never known anyone—except possibly your late mother—who is possessed of a more benevolent nature. You are always thinking of the other person—or creature! The much-cherished cross you gave to me. The newspaper accounts for me. The solicitousness for Mrs. Williamson. Do you never think of yourself?"

"Of course I do. It's just that I derive my most satisfying pleasure when I am able to help others."

"I pray I can learn from you. It will be my pleasure to collect you tomorrow and take you to the Williamson cottage."

Chapter 4

"As much as I adore having the Balfour family here," the elder Mrs. St. Vincent said when they removed to the drawing room after dinner, "I know you'll have to rush home before the snow falls any heavier."

Georgianne's brows collapsed, and she effected a pout. "I was so hoping Miss Elizabeth and Miss Catherine would sing for us."

"I have no intention of depriving us of so joyous an occurrence." Mrs. St. Vincent bestowed a glowing smile upon Cathy, then addressed Elizabeth. "Pray, will you not honor us with a song?"

Elizabeth shyly peered into her lap ever so briefly, then rose and elegantly strolled to the pianoforte. Half way there, she spoke to David. "I beg that you play while I sing."

He rose. "It will be my pleasure."

Truth be told, all of the St. Vincent's were more musically talented than the vicar's musical family.

While they were selecting the music, Cathy took the opportunity to speak with Mrs. St. Vincent, of whom she was vastly fond. She could never be in the woman's company and not wonder how so small a woman had given birth to two such tall sons. Because of her short stature, Mrs. St. Vincent gave the appearance that she was. . .well, there was no polite way to say it. She was rotund. Had she a longer frame, she would certainly have appeared thinner.

Clearly, her sons did not favor her physically. But David, at least, had inherited his mother's intelligence and geniality. Michael was a dear, but David had always been Cathy's favorite. She wondered if it was because his personality so resembled his mother's.

"I understand you're just back from visiting your daughter and grandchildren," Cathy began.

"Indeed. It was so difficult for me to leave the little darlings—I've three grandchildren now, you know—but the knowledge that my dear David would be home for Christmas was a perfect lure to bring me home."

"It *is* wonderful to have him home."

"I pray he never leaves again. If only he would purchase Belford Manor and settle down." Her gaze flitted to Michael, and her mouth folded into a grim line. "I pray, too, that Michael and his lovely wife are blessed with children. It's been two years now, and still no sign of babes. At this rate, David will become a father before him."

When Mrs. St. Vincent, a smile on her pink-cheeked face, turned to watch Elizabeth sing, Cathy felt a stab of jealousy. For the first time in her life, she was actually jealous of the sister she loved so dearly. All because Mrs. St. Vincent peered at Elizabeth almost simultaneously with speaking of David settling down and having a family.

Had he told his mother he intended to marry Elizabeth?

The dinner she had just consumed squirmed in Cathy's now-upset stomach as she, too, watched her lovely sister standing beside David as he played the pianoforte. What a beautiful couple they made, Elizabeth all delicate fairness and David so large and dark and powerful. She thought of tales of yore with knights rescuing fair maidens. What a perfect fair maiden Elizabeth would have made. And no man could improve upon David as a knight who gallantly rescued maidens in distress.

Even if Cathy was at this moment jealous of her sister, she had to admit she was possessed of a nightingale's lovely voice. Everyone in the chamber was mesmerized by the incredible beauty they saw and heard.

Most especially Lord Neely.

With her flirty ways at dinner, Elizabeth had won the viscount's admiration, now she appeared to have made a complete conquest of the titled visitor.

Would David also worship at Elizabeth's shrine? Cathy pulled her gaze away from the beautiful singer and watched him. It was difficult to tell how he felt about Elizabeth because his reading of the music required his full attention.

Cathy was compelled to stare at her sister. Elizabeth shone like diamond. She would peer into his lordship's eyes when words of love fell from her lips, then she would completely ignore him in order to flutter her lashes at David while smiling down at him.

Which of the two men did her sister favor?

It was impossible to tell. One moment every person in the chamber would swear she had fallen for Lord Neely; the next, one would be convinced marriage to David was imminent.

Elizabeth was also a consummate actress. Cathy folded her arms across her chest and glared.

Mrs. St. Vincent would know if David hoped to marry Elizabeth. Her heart thudding, her insides trembling with dread, Cathy's gaze shifted to David's mother. And her heart sank. Mrs. St. Vincent smiled happily on her son and Elizabeth.

Until now, it had never occurred to Cathy that her sister could be in love with David. How could she have been so completely stupid?

Cathy studied her sister, trying to determine if Elizabeth had, indeed, fallen in love with David. The very thought caused the contents of her stomach to flip. Yet she was powerless to look away from the beautiful couple. When Elizabeth's sparkling sapphire eyes caressed David, Cathy thought she would burst into tears.

Both of us are in love with the same man.

Cathy knew the secret of her own heart must lie buried.

When the song was finished, Elizabeth and David drew great applause.

"Now you, my dear," Mrs. St. Vincent said to Cathy, "you must honor us with a song."

Cathy prayed her voice would not quiver when she spoke, prayed she would not burst into tears. "Perhaps next time. We really must go before the snow begins to fall any heavier. And, I must confess, I'm not feeling quite the thing."

David's brows lowered, and he moved to her. "Allow me to fetch your cloak."

After he procured her cloak and they faced each other in the entry hall, he said, "You can't go to the Williamson cottage in the morning if you're ill."

She was thankful he was giving her the perfect excuse to cancel the morning's outing. Knowing that Elizabeth might be in love with him—and he might return that love—Cathy would never be comfortable planning anything with him that would exclude her sister. Her heart aching, she looked up into his earnest face. "I don't suppose I can go." She offered him a wan smile. "You, my dear captain, will now be free to enjoy your visitor tomorrow."

He shrugged. "I shall be uneasy about you."

Before she could respond, Elizabeth came up to them. "I declare, pet, you are never ill. I shall be quite worried about you."

"A day's rest and I daresay I'll be back to my meddling self."

Elizabeth looked up at David. "I just cannot credit it. I am the one with the delicate constitution. I shall be vexed to no end with worry for my little sister."

Elizabeth began to assist David with helping Cathy don her pelisse and heavy woolen cloak, then met David's gaze. "I have neglected to tell you, Captain, how appreciative I am of your accompaniment."

His black eyes shimmered as he gazed affectionately at her. "It is I who should be thanking you—as should everyone in that chamber—for singing so beautifully for all of us."

"Indeed," Lord Neely added as he strolled up to Elizabeth as the servant was bringing her cloak. The viscount took it and draped it over Elizabeth's milky bare shoulders. "You sing like an angel."

She thanked him, curtseying. "Will we see you at the Christmas Eve Assembly?"

"I daresay I shall see you before that. Will you do me the goodness of allowing me to call on you?"

Her gaze skipped from him, to David, then back to him. "I adore having callers."

During the jostling carriage ride home, Cathy felt even sicker. She refrained from engaging her sister in conversation but listened to her prattle on about how delightful was Lord Neely, how handsome was David.

Prattling along as rapidly as Elizabeth, Aunt Kate was over the moon, singing the praises of the young, *bachelor* viscount.

Nothing in Elizabeth's responses, though, provided any enlightenment about her preference between the two men.

If Elizabeth should be in love with David, Cathy knew she would have to step aside and bless the union. She loved both of them most dearly.

Why had it never occurred to her that Elizabeth, too, could be in love with the irresistibly handsome Captain David St. Vincent? She supposed Aunt Kate had done a thorough job all these years of convincing her that Elizabeth would wed a title.

But surely no one could prefer the dandyish Lord Neely over the supremely masculine Captain David St. Vincent.

When they reached Stoneyway, Cathy went straight to the bedchamber she shared with her sister—and Fluffs, who always slept with Cathy. Elizabeth made a great fuss over her. She personally stoked the fire, and she took one of the blankets off her bed to spread over Cathy, who was now shivering. "Oh, my dearest," she murmured sweetly, "I shall be prostrate if my little lamb of a sister is not completely well come morning."

It was at times like this Cathy recalled her

childhood, when Elizabeth had always been her staunchest champion. In recent years, their rolls had rather reversed, owing to Elizabeth's dependent personality—and Cathy's greater maturity.

When Elizabeth's tenderness shone through as it did tonight, Cathy knew she would do anything in her power to see to it her sister married the man of her dreams.

Even if that man were David.

Faint sunlight filtered into her bedchamber the following morning. Even though the fire had died, she was warm beneath a mountain of blankets. And she felt good.

Until she clearly recalled that her sister might also be in love with the man she loved. Then, with a woefully sinking feeling returning to the pit of her stomach, she recalled, too, that David's mother must be privy to the information that her son wished to settle down with the beautiful Balfour sister.

Cathy could not allow herself to continue lying in bed, dwelling on her melancholy thoughts. Especially not when Mrs. Williamson might need her. She left her bed and quickly threw the woolen cloak about her to protect her from the room's chill as she hurried to the window and fully opened the curtains. A smile crossed her face. The sporadic snow had stopped, and the sun was straining to gain strength in the eastern sky. She would go to Mrs. Williamson's.

How low it made her to think that she could have ridden to Mrs. Williamson's in a warm carriage with the dashing captain. Except she could not. Not if Elizabeth loved him. Not if he were in love with Elizabeth.

As she stood there on the cold stone floors peering out the frosty window, Elizabeth brought her a cup of hot tea. "I heard you stirring, love. How are you feeling this morning?"

Cathy turned to gaze at the sister who had spoken so tenderly to her. Elizabeth was fully dressed—to Cathy's surprise in a warm, woolen frock of deep green. "I am back to normal. Thank you for the tea."

"Why do you not climb back into bed? You must be freezing in your bare feet."

Cathy shook her head. "I hope to be on the road by the time the sun is fully up."

"You cannot be serious! You're planning to walk all that way to the Williamson cottage?"

"I am."

"My dear sister, are you aware that it is winter? And this happens to be one of the coldest days of the year?"

Cathy giggled. "I am aware."

"I don't think Papa will approve."

"Papa will approve. It's exactly the kind of thing Mama would have done, and you know Papa thinks Mama was completely without fault."

Elizabeth frowned. "I haven't worried so about you since you were a girl."

"Because I've developed into a competent, pragmatic woman who does not do foolish things." *Except for falling in love with a man who was probably in love with her sister.*

"In most respects, that is true. But I cannot say my competent sister never does foolish things when she insists upon sacrificing her own good health in service to others."

Cathy was unbelievably moved by her sister's

concern. "Don't worry so. I'm leaving early in the day so I can return well before the late afternoon chill bears down on us."

"It's a pity we have no carriage."

"Not having ever had one, it's not something I miss." She found herself wondering if David's newly found fortune would extend to the purchase of a carriage. What was it to her? He was sure to declare himself to the loveliest girl in all the shire.

David did not like it at all. Lord Neely was besotted over the woman David had loved most of his life. Because he had neither declared himself nor had any understanding with the young lady, David could hardly have objected when his lordship insisted on paying a call at Stoneyway.

His brother and sister-in-law had begged off that afternoon. He appreciated that they did so to allow room in the sleigh for the bachelors to take the Balfour sisters on a sleigh ride.

During many a broiling day in the West Indies, he had imagined himself galloping through the snow with the beautiful Miss Balfour beside him.

The notion of bundling beneath a rug with Miss Elizabeth Balfour as they sped across the snow held great appeal, but he would rather not go at all than to see her seated beside the viscount.

It was a pity that being in love could make a perfectly rational man take a dislike to another man he had previously found to be amiable.

Save for his new-found obsession over Elizabeth Balfour, Lord Neely was a man David admired. He neither flaunted his aristocratic lineage nor boasted on his vast land holdings. He was kindly, generous, and intelligent. He was dashed good at whist—and an even better a shot than David, who was acknowledged to be uncommonly skilled with a musket.

As they raced across the icy fields, Lord Neely at the ribbons, David had to begrudgingly credit the viscount with being a notable whip.

Were it not for Elizabeth Balfour—who had admitted she wished to marry a titled gentleman—David would have been proud to count the viscount as his friend.

"It's a pity for Miss Balfour she's hidden away in Cumbria," Lord Neely said. "Were she to have a Season in Town, I daresay she would outshine every lady in London."

"You refer, then, to Miss Elizabeth Balfour?" David knew very well the viscount was speaking of the prettier sister. His arms folded stiffly across his chest, his mouth clamped into a firm line, David stared ahead at the powdery white snow that carpeted this countryside he loved so thoroughly.

"Yes, of course. I say, St. Vincent, is there an understanding between you and Miss Catherine Balfour?"

Cathy? "Of course not! Why would you think such a thing?"

The viscount shrugged. "It just seemed to me the girl was excessively fond of you, and I thought you might feel the same."

"She's little more than a child! Of course I hold her in great affection since I've known her since she was born, but it's an altogether different affection than. . . " He almost said *than I feel for Elizabeth.* "Than I would feel for one with whom I had an understanding."

He wanted to warn Lord Neely away from

Elizabeth. All he had to say was that he planned to ask for her hand, and as a gentleman, Lord Neely would back away. But David was incapable of sharing something so intimate with another man.

He had no assurances Elizabeth would even accept his suit. And what if she had fallen for the viscount? As difficult as it would be, he wanted her to have a clear choice between the two men. And he wanted her to be happy.

If he was going to spend the rest of his life with one woman, it must be with a woman who wanted to spend the rest of her life with him—and no other.

Once they arrived at Stoneyway, Elizabeth and her aunt joined them in the drawing room. It was the first time she had not worn a dress that displayed her creamy shoulders and the sweet way her breasts separated just above the bodice. It was actually the first time he had seen her dress sensibly. Like Cathy.

It struck him that the sister who was three years younger was by far the more mature. "Where is Miss Catherine?" he asked.

Elizabeth elegantly lowered herself onto the sofa, rolling her eyes. "My sister insisted on visiting that poor Williamson widow."

It was far too cold for a lone girl to go off on foot like that! "Then I trust she has recovered fully from last night's indisposition?"

"Apparently so." Elizabeth turned to address Lord Neely. "How did you find today's weather, my lord?"

"It's cold, but if one is properly covered, it's pleasant enough. We came in the sleigh."

Her eyes shimmered. "That sounds delightful."

David tried to determine if she was attracted to the viscount. The way she smiled at him was full of affection, but it was the same when she smiled at David.

"Perhaps when your sister returns we could take a sleigh ride," Lord Neely said.

"I should like that ever so much."

"When do you expect your sister to return?" the viscount asked.

"One never knows. She could be back very soon, but if the widow is low, Cathy won't leave until she cheers her." She shrugged. "I don't know how Cathy can stand to go to that dingy little cottage! I would be afraid to sit down there."

David eyed Lord Neely. "The woman's husband was a coal miner." He did wish Elizabeth was. . . more like Cathy.

His lordship nodded. "Oh, I expect there's coal dust everywhere."

"I expect it's the devil to get out of the upholstered furniture," David said in defense of a woman he'd never met.

Elizabeth scrunched up her perfect nose. "Indeed. I, for one, will never set foot inside that cottage again."

So, David thought, Cathy was not only the more mature sister, she was the more charitable. He looked to the aunt to see if she would chastise Elizabeth, but the woman merely cast an adoring glance at her niece.

"Changing the conversation to a happier topic," Lord Neely said, "tomorrow's Christmas Eve."

"I cannot wait for the assembly!" Elizabeth eyed the viscount. "I cannot tell you, my lord, how honored our community will be to have you attend."

"The honor is mine, Miss Balfour. Would I be presumptuous if I asked permission to lead you out for the first dance?"

Who did he think he was, waltzing in here and claiming the prettiest girl in the entire shire? David felt like poking him in the eye.

Her lashes did that fluttering thing that made men's heartbeats accelerate. "I should be exceedingly honored, my lord."

"It's I who am honored, Miss Balfour. Allow me to say how happy I am that I chose to spend Christmas with my old friend Michael St. Vincent."

David's gaze swept again to the girls' aunt. She sat there with her sewing, looking for all the world like she'd just been crowned queen. If she were a man, David would like to poke her in the eye, too, for filling her niece's head with dreams of marrying a title.

Elizabeth sighed! David could not recall her ever sighing when he spoke to her. "Do you believe in fate, my lord?" she asked, looking dreamily at him.

"Before yesterday I would have said no."

The audacity! They were carrying on a flirtation right in front of him. "I will own," David said, "I thought it must be ordained by fate that when I returned from a six-year absence I found Miss Balfour still remained unmarried." Good Lord! What was he doing? It sounded suspiciously as if he *were* declaring himself.

"I assure you," the spinster aunt said, glaring at David, "my niece has had many opportunities to wed, but she was saving herself for someone more grand than is generally found in Ramseyfield." Miss Kate Balfour cast an affectionate glance at Lord Neely.

But Miss Elizabeth Balfour bestowed a stupendous smile upon David. "You will surely turn my head, Captain! I declare, it's fate, too, that despite all the dangers that surrounded you, you survived that awful war and have now come home to us."

In that instant, David forgot that she'd been flirting with Lord Neely. At that instant, he felt as if the beautiful Elizabeth Balfour had just declared her love to him.

Miss Balfour, the viscount, and the aunt continued to converse, but he couldn't have repeated a word they said. Only the words she'd just spoken to him, the way she had gazed so adoringly at him dominated his thoughts.

Then he recalled how she had also spoken so sweetly to Lord Neely. And was it not to Lord Neely that she had first tossed out her allusion to *fate*? How could one young woman feel so connected by fate to *two* gentlemen? Was it possible for a woman to be in love with two men?

He felt like a bird shot in flight. A woman could only marry one man. And David wanted to be assured the woman he married was in love with only him.

The front door to Stoneyway burst open, and since the door that separated the drawing room from the entry hall was open, he saw Cathy.

And he leapt to his feet. "What in the blazes has happened to you?"

Chapter 5

Miss Catherine Balfour could not believe one more piece of misfortune had been heaped upon her. The one day the door to the drawing was left open just happened to be when a pair of gentlemen callers—including THE only one she could ever care to impress—had to be witness to her bedraggled self limping into Stoneyway's entry hall looking for all the world as if a steady stream of mud had rained down upon her.

Which wasn't far from the truth of what had occurred.

When she had seen the sleigh in front of Stoneyway, she had instinctively known it would be David, and she had given serious consideration to hiding herself from view until he left. But she was absurdly uncomfortable. And cold. And miserable. She, therefore, convinced herself the drawing room door would be shut as it usually was when they had visitors, which would allow her to quietly enter the house and steal up the stairs without being seen.

How mortified she had been after she entered the house and her gaze swung to the drawing room—and to David's shocked expression.

"Cathy!" He bolted toward the stairway she was attempting to climb. "What's happened to you?"

Elizabeth followed on his heels. Her sister's cries succeeded in prying Mr. Balfour from his library. "Whatever has happened to my daughter?"

It was her father's pitying gaze that dropped Cathy to her mud-encrusted knees, hiding her weeping face in her cupped hands. How could she tell them how foolish she'd been? The always-pragmatic Catherine Balfour had been so despondent by the realization that the man she loved was probably going to marry her sister that she had been completely oblivious to where she was walking after she left Mrs. Williamson's. She did not see the drop-off of the lane upon which she was traveling. The drop-off went straight into a ravine that was scored with hawthorn bushes and which had been disturbed by burrowing badgers, who'd dug beneath the snow to expose wet, black dirt.

Lacerations from the hawthorn branches were the least of her woes. Every garment upon her bruised body was torn, wet, and muddy. Though she could not see it, she knew her face, too, was likely black—and bloody.

"Pray, it is nothing," she managed between sobs.

"It most certainly is something," her father bellowed. "I demand that you tell me what happened."

By this time, Elizabeth had returned with a wet cloth and set about to gently remove the blood and mud from her sister's face—a face Cathy insisted on turning *away* from the eyes of the three men who gawked at her. "Mrs. Greenhampton is heating water for you a bath," Elizabeth murmured.

"I wasn't watching where I was going, and I fell into the ravine that runs behind the Minton cottage." Cathy fully expected the gentlemen callers to laugh at her foolishness. If not at her appearance.

Neither did.

"Pray, love," Elizabeth asked, "have you broken anything?"

Cathy shook her head, still not desiring to meet David's gaze, praying he wouldn't see how terrible she looked but knowing he did. "I assure you, I am unhurt."

"Why is she bleeding?" Mr. Balfour asked.

David came to settle on the lowest step. Through a slender gap between the fingers which covered her humiliated face, she saw that he looked up at her with concern, though all she could think of was how horrid she looked. "I perceive that you must have met resistance from a shrub of some sort." His voice was incredibly gentle.

She sniffed. And nodded. "Indeed."

"Allow me to examine the wounds," he said. "I've had some experience with this sort of thing."

There was no way she was going to allow him the opportunity to further observe her in the state she was in. Especially when her perfectly perfect looking sister was right next to her. She shook her head adamantly and attempted to regain the stridency to her voice. But she still would not look at him. "I assure you, most of the bruising has been to my pride."

"Oh, my dearest!" Elizabeth exclaimed. "My poor sister does not want you gentlemen to see her looking so . . . so . . ." Elizabeth obviously did not want to state the obvious: *My sister doesn't want you to see her looking so ugly.*

"So perfectly UNlovely," Cathy finished for her polite sister.

"You are *not* unlovely," Elizabeth crooned. "You need only to take a bath and get on fresh clothes." She turned to address the gentlemen. "It doesn't look as if my sister and I will be able to go sleigh riding with you today. I am most anxious to assure myself my poor sister is not hurt worse than she says. She tends to minimize any injuries to herself."

David stood. "Yes, of course, she will be much better once she's upstairs with you."

Lord Neely came to stand beside David and peer up at the sisters. "It will be my pleasure to call for you ladies in my carriage tomorrow evening to take you to the assembly."

"I should adore that," Elizabeth responded, "but I have promised to come early and help set up."

"I have no aversion to going early," his lordship said.

"Then I will be ever so delighted to have you gentlemen call for us."

Cathy shook her head. "Not me."

"Now, pet," Elizabeth said, "you don't know that you won't be perfectly well by tomorrow. You said yourself, you're not hurt."

"It's not that. I. . . w-w-ill. . .be. . . fine. It's just that I won't be able to go early with you because I plan to be returning from Mrs. Williamson's at that time."

"Surely you aren't planning to go to that filthy cottage on Christmas Eve!" Elizabeth protested.

"If she feels up to it," their father said, his voice stern, "I see no reason why she shouldn't go on Christmas Eve, and I see many reasons why she should."

"Yes, of course, Papa." Elizabeth's voice was

barely above a whisper.

"Then I'll send my brother's carriage to collect you later, Miss Balfour," David said to Cathy.

"I would be most appreciative for a ride on a cold evening." With that, she scrambled up the stairs.

A warm bath, clean clothing, and a good night's sleep and Cathy was nearly recovered from the previous day's debacle. The skin on her left knee had suffered a good scraping, but if she didn't bend it too much, she ought to be able to manage the walk to and from the Williamson cottage.

Even though her face would never be pretty like Elizabeth's, she was grateful it had escaped the cuts which seemed to cover most of her body. She had told herself that if her face were bruised, she would not go to tonight's assembly and be a laughingstock. Despite that she expected to be somewhat of a wallflower, she greatly looked forward to attending the Christmas Eve assembly. It was always a festive and joyous occasion.

She bundled up as warmly as possible and set off for the Williamson cottage. How grateful she was the winds were not strong that day. As much as she enjoyed walking through the countryside, she very much disliked doing so when chill winds cut into her. Because she was a stout walker, Cathy could cover the four and half miles—which included a good bit of uphill walking—between their houses in an hour.

When she arrived at the Williamson cottage, there was no answer to her knock.

But she heard moans.

The babe is coming! Cathy tried the door

handle, and it opened. The sounds of a woman suffering were much more distinct once she was inside the house. Cathy's heartbeat accelerated. She was going to have to assist at the birth!

Only once before had she been allowed into a birthing chamber: just months before Mama had died, she had taken Cathy with her and calmly explained everything to her, alleviating her initial fears. Had Mama known her youngest daughter would soon be called upon to step into her shoes?

"Mrs. Williamson?"

"I. Am. Here. In the bedchamber."

Cathy began to tremble as she strode to the next room. It was still dark. She went straight to the rumpled bed and gazed down at the suffering woman. "How long has it been?" she asked as she stroked a gentle hand across the woman's moist brow.

"Since dawn."

"My mother said first babes take longer than subsequent children. I pray yours doesn't take twenty hours—as did my elder sister."

Mrs. Williamson tried to chuckle, but was seized by a gripping shot of pain.

Cathy took her hand and held it. "Everything will be fine. I am here with you now."

She had never been so scared.

Miss Elizabeth Balfour was the belle of the ball. David had never seen her lovelier. After Neely claimed her for the first dance, David was honored to stand up with her for the second.

Oddly enough, it wasn't her beautiful face he wanted most to behold. He kept picturing Cathy, her sweet face buried in her hands, as she'd looked when he had last seen her. Now he was even more uneasy about her than he had been on the previous day.

Instead of standing with the army of Elizabeth Balfour's admirers gazing longingly at her, he kept finding himself watching the door. When was Cathy going to arrive? He had sent his family's carriage to collect her more than an hour ago. Stoneyway was less than a mile from the assembly hall. She should have been here by now.

What if she had fallen again while returning from the Williamson cottage? What if she had plunged into the frozen river? The very idea was like knife to his gut.

Then he would attempt to be logical. The reason for her delay could easily be explained. The most likely explanation was that Mrs. Williamson's babe was coming today, and Cathy was staying to assist the unfortunate widow.

Yet when he told himself that was the most plausible reason why she had not come, he still could not stop worrying about her.

It suddenly occurred to him this assembly was meaningless to him without the presence of Miss Catherine Balfour. He raced to his brother, who was talking to a group of male neighbors. "I'm uneasy about Cathy Balfour. I sent your coach to collect her at Stoneyway more than hour ago."

Michael's brows lowered. "That's only half a mile from here!"

"I know. I'm going to see what I can find out."

"Take Neely's coach so you won't have to walk through the snow in those clothes."

David was so alarmed about Cathy, he hadn't even considered his own comfort, but he was grateful Neely's coach would be available to him.

It took less than five minutes to reach

Stoneyway, but when he did, his heart fell. Not a single window was lighted. In front of the dark stone cottage sat his brother's coach, the coachman on the box.

And there was no sign of Cathy.

Chapter 6

David had hopped up on the box beside his brother's coachman and directed him to the Williamson cottage. Riding on top would allow him to better search the countryside for signs of Cathy—if she were out there alone in the wilderness.

It would be bloody difficult to see anything, though. Night had fallen, and it was a black night with barely a sliver of moon notched into the darkness that wrapped around them. A thin coating of snow covered the ground, making everything black, white, or an eerie gray.

His thundering heartbeat rhythmically pounded with each hoof printing the crunchy snow. He had requested the driver follow along the river, though he'd been incapable of giving voice to his worst fear: that Cathy may have fallen into the swollen, frigid waterway.

Dread filling him like a vile poison, he kept remembering how pitiable she had looked when he last saw her, kept remembering how worried he had been about her, kept remembering that he'd wanted to draw her into his arms and comfort her. What if she had stumbled again?

He was reminded, too, of that first evening he'd returned to Ramseyfield and of the lone young woman pushing through the snowdrifts that wretched night. The strong-willed, big-hearted, foolhardy, maddening girl should have more regard for her own wellbeing!

"It be a mighty cold night, guvnah."

Until the coachman spoke, David had not realized how badly his ears stung or how numb with cold his hands were. He hadn't given a second's consideration to his own discomfort because his fears for Cathy outweighed everything else. "Yes, it is."

His feeling of unease had begun back at the assembly. There he had stood, surrounded by those people he had known all his life, the people he loved best, yet he'd been melancholy. Why was he not happy to be home, happy to be surrounded by those who meant so much to him? Suddenly he had realized that the person who meant most to him wasn't there.

The face he cherished most did not belong to Elizabeth Balfour. It belonged to her younger sister.

Cathy was the truly beautiful sister for she was beautiful on the inside. And wasn't that what counted above everything? She was perhaps the most admirable person he had ever known. She possessed a rare ability to make those around her feel as if they were the most important person in her life. He most certainly was not singular in that belief. He supposed she even had the same effect upon the dogs and cats she fussed over.

But I know I am special to her.

Hadn't she once confessed that she wanted to wed him? His pulse pounded. Dare he hope she still felt the same?

She had followed his naval career with a keen interest. She had admitted that she worried about his safety during the years of his absence. Could he allow himself to hope he was the only man who could win her heart?

Could he actually be in love with Cathy Balfour? Was love what made his worries spread over him, sickening his whole body like some vile poison? Was love what made *her* face the only one that could gladden his heart?

It suddenly became abundantly clear to him that he could navigate the globe and never find a woman who could mean more to him than Cathy. Her equal could not be found in another city, country, or continent.

When he finally saw the Williamson cottage off in the distance, his heartbeat accelerated. He knew it was the Williamson cottage though all he could see of it in this darkest of nights was a buttery square of light. He prayed she would be there.

It seemed as if these last five hundred yards took as long to traverse as the five miles they had already covered. Would they never reach the cottage?

The coachman must have sensed David's urgency for he never let up on the speed as he brought the coach almost up to the front door of the little stone cottage.

David leapt from the box, raced to the weathered timber door, and knocked.

The door opened slowly. Then he saw Cathy.

And hauled her into his arms.

Chapter 7

Nothing in her entire nineteen years had ever felt so good as being wrapped in David's strong embrace. When she peered up into his face, wondering what she could possibly have done to deserve such happiness, she discovered something even better.

His mouth closed over hers, gently at first, then after her ardent response, he kissed her more hungrily. It was as if she were in one of her own dreams! She had often dreamed of finding herself in David's arms. But David in the flesh—a real, live, warm, musky smelling, heavily breathing David—was so much better than any of her dreams had ever been!

She knew they stood there in the open doorway. She knew it was a chilling night. But she felt nothing but warmth.

And overwhelmingly love.

Until this moment she had never realized how intimately a kiss connected two people. She experienced the oddest sensation that their two beings were merging into one. She thought of the words her father read from Scripture when he presided over weddings. Dare she even allow her thoughts to drift in that direction?

When the kiss finally terminated, he continued to hold her close. "My dearest Cathy, I've been so worried about you."

Her first coherent thought was. . . *He is not in*

love with my sister. She could hallelujah! the heavens.

She had no desire to respond for fear he would come to his senses, beg her forgiveness, and storm away because this had all been some terribly disappointing mistake. Instead, her arms encircled his powerful body, and she nestled the side of her face into his broad chest.

"I have no right to do this," he murmured, "yet nothing I've ever done has felt more right."

Her hold tightened. Still, she said nothing. When she was twelve and half, she had tossed pride to the wind and declared her love to him. Nothing had changed—except her resolve to not humiliate herself—even if it was painfully difficult not to tell him he was the only man she would ever love.

"I know I've only been home a few days, but I know my feelings for you are deep, and they are irreversible. I know that I could circumnavigate the world and never find a woman I could love as much as I love you, Catherine Balfour."

"Oh, David," was all she could say before she started to weep.

Then she remembered poor Mrs. Williamson. "Oh, David, will you send the coachman to fetch the midwife over in Cloverling?"

He pulled back, his firm hands planted at her shoulders, his dark brows lowered. "Not until you tell me why you're crying. Have I offended you, my dearest love?"

Her tears gushed. She really wished they wouldn't because then her eyes would get all red, and she'd look ugly, and she didn't want to look ugly, not when David made her feel as if she were as lovely as. . .as lovely as Elizabeth. She did so want David to think her pretty. She shook her head. "It's just that you've made me very happy."

His hands still gripped her shoulders, but ever so gently, and his thumbs began to sweep into gentle circles against her flesh. "Happy enough to become my wife?"

She launched herself once more into his arms. "Oh, yes! I told you I'd wait."

At dawn, he heard the babe's cry. He had stayed at the Williamson cottage, seeing that the fires did not burn out. During the previous night, he had sent the poor coachman crisscrossing the countryside. The coachman had not only brought back the midwife, but he had also gone to tell Mr. Balfour that his younger daughter was safe at the home of Mrs. Williamson, whose time had come. Then later, David sent the coachman back to Rosemary Hill to deliver a quickly scribbled letter to Michael—and ordered the coachman to stay home and spend Christmas morning with his loved ones.

David's letter notified his brother of his pending nuptials but asked that he not tell anyone until David received official permission from the vicar.

David was determined to be with his beloved on this Christmas morning, their first together. He was so filled with joy. Cathy loved him! Cathy had agreed to marry him. He never wanted to ever again separate from her. Not even to go back to Rosemary Hill.

That the babe's cry was lusty must give comfort to its mother for she'd obviously given birth to a healthy child. The babe would not only give comfort, but it would also dispel her loneliness.

A moment later, an exhausted looking Cathy slipped out of the room and faced him with a smile on her face. "Mrs. Williamson has a fine son. He's sleeping now in his mother's arms."

She moved to him, and his arm naturally draped over her shoulder. "Has she given him a name?"

Cathy nodded, then somberly answered. "Frederick."

As a lad, Frederick Williamson had been a playmate of David's. How happy it made him that part of his old friend would live on in this child.

"This shall be my favorite ever Christmas," she whispered.

"Mine, too. Your love is the most precious of gifts."

"I feel the same, and I believe Mrs. Williamson will come to realize what a wondrous Christmas gift she has been given."

His heart swelled with love of Cathy, with thoughts of the children they would one day have, with how privileged he was to return to Ramseyfield and settle down with this remarkable woman.

CHAPTER 8

One year later...

David had thought last Christmas his happiest, especially coming as it did after so many years when he'd been deprived of his loving family. How happy he'd been just to be home for Christmas. Then, the most perfect of beings had consented to become his wife.

But this year's Christmas was even better. He and his wife sat there in the family pew at the Christmas morning service. How their families had expanded! He cast a quick glance at Cathy. How he loved to see her holding their sleeping daughter. How dearly he and Cath had come to love little Charlotte in the two short months they had been parents.

Then his gaze swept to Cathy's pretty sister, now Lady Neely. Elizabeth looked lovingly at the son who lay sleeping in her arms.

Across the aisle were Michael and Georgianne with their twins, a boy and a girl, who ironically had been born just a week before Charlotte.

When Cathy's father cleared his throat, David's gaze returned to the pulpit. Her normally reticent Papa had difficulty disguising his pride when he looked at his family. Though Cathy had worried when she and Elizabeth both left the nest at the same time, she no longer worried about her father being lonely.

David's gaze flicked to his mother, who now shared the Balfour family pew. She and Mr. Balfour had united in marriage during the past year and were supremely compatible.

Even the widow Williamson, her sturdy little son balancing on her hip, had proudly told Cathy on the steps of the church that morning that no one ever had a finer Christmas gift than the laddie she received on the previous Christmas.

After church, all the family would gather at Belford Manor, the beautiful home David had bought as Cathy's wedding gift.

Now he had truly come home for Christmas.

The End

Christmas At Farley Manor

Cheryl Bolen

Copyright © 2011 by Cheryl Bolen

Christmas At Farley Manor is a work of fiction. Names, characters, places, and incidents are the products of the author's imagination or are used fictitiously. Any resemblance to actual events, locales, or persons, living or dead, is entirely coincidental.

All rights reserved.

No part of this publication may be reproduced, stored or transmitted in any form or by any means without the prior written permission of the author.

Prologue

London, 1812

Captain Harry Tate did not know why he felt compelled to tether his mount and limp into St. Clement's that morning. Quite clearly, it was another sign he would soon be meeting his Maker. He still could not believe he hadn't died at Badajoz along with hundreds of his men. God, but he could still smell their burning flesh, still hear the death cries of men who had served under him, still picture the mounds of mutilated bodies. Good English soldiers.

He was but five and twenty years of age, but he knew in his heart he would not live to twenty-six. For he would return to the Peninsula on the morrow. It was his duty. The words of the slain Lord Nelson were in the minds and hearts of all Englishmen. "England expects that every man will do his duty." His leg was finally healing. He must return.

It was almost as if death had followed him to London. For Annie was dead now, too. Beautiful Annie who'd sung her silly songs on the stage with every man in the audience lusting after her. Yet it was he who'd won her affections, he who had become her protector, he who had killed her.

He meant to say a prayer for sweet, loving Annie, whose dancing eyes were closed forever. The huge timber doors squeaked as he opened them. Though the church was dark, the crucifix at the front of the church seemed illuminated, beckoning him down the nave to the sacristy. He knelt at the altar rail and began to pray for Annie's soul.

As well as his own.

Then he realized he was not alone. A soft whimpering was very close. Had Annie's distraught friend followed him? He spun around. A very pretty young blonde he'd never seen before sat weeping on the front row.

He went to her. She was dressed as a gentlewoman. "Pray, is there something I can do to assist you?"

Her gaze lifted and swept over his regimentals as her head shook before she buried her lovely face in her hands.

What in the blazes should he do? He could not force himself on the poor girl, but he could not leave her like this, either. She could not be more than twenty and looked as if—well, she looked as low as he felt.

Captain Harry Tate was too accustomed to commanding. "Miss, I'm quite sure things cannot be as bad as. . ." Then he thought of what could make one so low. "Pray, have you lost a loved one?"

She shook her head, her face still buried in her delicate hands.

Then—if one were keeping score—he was more unfortunate than she because he *had recently* lost a loved one. Not to mention all his men who'd died in battle. "Then things can't be all that bad."

"Oh, but they most decidedly are," she said in a cultured voice. This lady was no doxie.

She must be pregnant. That was it! He could see she wore no wedding ring.

The poor creature must have been thrown out of her home. Perhaps he *could* help her. He was, after all, the son of a viscount. Any number of resources—not the least of which was financial—were at his disposal. Surely there was something he could do to dispel this poor creature's gloom. "I am not going to leave this church until you tell me what distresses you so. I may be able to offer assistance."

"I think not," she managed in a strident voice. "You, sir, are a man, and at present I am out of charity with men!"

She is pregnant. And even with her pale blue eyes swimming in red, she was a stunner.

Captain Harry Tate did not make idle threats. He sat next to her, his spine stiff, his arms folded across his chest. "I will not leave until you reveal to me the nature of your distress."

She said nothing. She blew her nose into a lace handkerchief, and it appeared as if her tears had quite vanished. They both sat there silently in their own sorrowful states, staring at the crucifix.

When it appeared she was not going to speak to him, he decided to initiate a conversation. "As it happens, miss, I *have* recently lost a loved one. I regret that I could not have been with her at the end. I feel culpable in her death. It might assuage my guilt if I can help another lady in distress. And I give you my vow, I'll not. . ." He lowered his voice. After all, this was the Lord's house. He disliked speaking of such in church, but he thought he must. "I vow I'll not try to . . .to take improper liberties. It's obvious you're a gentlewoman." Even if she had gotten herself pregnant.

Now her shoulders began to shake with more

sobs.

He was deuced unhappy about the poor girl. And since he knew he faced death in Spain, he had nothing to lose. "If your child needs a father, I will marry you before I leave tomorrow. Will that solve your problem?"

Her shoulders began to shake even harder, but now they shook with laughter! The chit was laughing at him.

Finally she dabbled at her eyes with that lacey handkerchief and looked squarely at him. "Sir, that is very gallant of you, but I am *not* in a family way."

His brows lowered. "You're not in the family way, and you haven't lost a loved one, what, pray tell, could cause you such distress?"

She hadn't meant to speak to him. He was, after all, a complete stranger. But he was also a gentleman. And now he had proven to be an honorable gentleman—the first she had encountered since her dear papa's death the previous year.

That this man would, first, vow not to seduce her, then so honorably offer marriage to a woman he'd never before seen was astonishing. What a kind soul he must be.

And how tortured he must be by the loss of his loved one. He obviously did not believe he would ever again find love. Which was very sad.

What a prize he would be for some fortunate woman. In her nineteen years, Elizabeth Hensley had never seen a more handsome specimen. And it was not just his alluring uniform on a tall, powerfully built body. He was possessed of dark brown hair and piercing black eyes. The finely sculpted lines of his patrician—and exceedingly attractive—face were softened by a deep cleft in his chin.

More than his good looks, though, this officer demonstrated a nobility of character.

She faced him, smiling. "You are very kind indeed, sir, to concern yourself with my well-being. I am sorry for your loss. My problems will seem insignificant compared to yours."

"Try me." His black eyes bore into hers.

She drew a deep breath. "I have spent the night in this church because I have nowhere else to go."

"Have you no family?"

She shook her head. "None. My father died last year. Because he was a poor country parson, there was only enough money left to last me until I could find a position as a governess."

"And you did?"

"Yes. I obtained a post in the house of a gentleman here in London."

"When was that?"

"Three months ago."

"But you are no longer employed at that house?"

"I fled in the middle of the night. Last night."

"I perceive the *gentleman* did not act like a gentleman?"

"Until he tried to sneak into my bedchamber last night, he had always conducted himself as a gentleman. But last night he was most contemptible."

"He didn't . . .?"

"No, he didn't. I told him if he didn't leave my bedchamber immediately I would scream so loud his wife and little girls would come running and judge his depravity. I waited half an hour after he left, then I gathered up my things and crept away from the house." She started to cry again.

He waited until she regained her composure, then asked, "And you have no money?'

"None."

"So, correct me if I'm wrong. You have no money. No home. And no family?"

She sniffed. "You are correct, sir. My mother and father were quite old when they became parents. They thought they would never have children." She smiled. "My mother was three and forty when I was born; my father was ten years older than she. They're both gone now."

"My dear lady, your problems are not so monumental. I believe the Lord must have led me to you today."

Her brows lowered. "What can you mean?" Surely he was not going to offer for her again. There was a limit to gallantry.

"Tell me," he said, "do you like children?"

What did that matter? "Of course I like children. I would be a most depraved creature did I not."

"What of babes?"

Her voice softened at the thought of holding a sleeping infant and stroking its soft downy hair. "Is there anything more precious? I will own, I have no experience with babes." Why was this man quizzing her about babies?

"Nor do I, but it seems I am now responsible for one." He had a responsibility to get the infant child away from those ladies of easy virtue.

The poor girl babe that Annie died giving life to was his.

Since he'd learned of Annie's death—and

subsequently learned of the existence of his child—he'd been equally as low knowing his child would likely be raised to be a courtesan. Kitty was willing to care for her closest friend's child—providing Harry compensate her appropriately. But providing materially for the child did little to assuage his conscience.

How he had wished he could have sent the little girl to live at Farley Manor, but Harry's father was an excessively stern man who would not tolerate his only son's bastards. And Harry could hardly care for the child himself.

He fully expected to be dead before a year had passed.

This lovely young gentlewoman was exactly what he needed, and he took some comfort in knowing he was what she needed.

"You are married, sir?"

He gave a bitter laugh. "As long as I'm in service to his majesty, I would not ask a woman to throw away her future on the likes of me." He turned to her. "After I return to the Peninsula tomorrow, I'm quite certain I shall never see England again."

"You cannot be certain of such a thing! Only God knows what's in store for any of us."

"Spoken like a rector's daughter. But be that as it may, I know my destiny. I feel death closing in all around me."

Those soft blue eyes of hers held him in her pitying gaze. "Pray, don't say such things! You're a young, able-bodied, quite noble man. Now tell me, why do you say the Lord led you here today?"

It pleased him that, in her concern for him, her personal melancholy had vanished. "Because you are exactly what I need, and I believe I am what you need."

The kindly expression on her lovely face turned to wariness. Surely the very young woman didn't think he meant to seduce her! She was a clergyman's daughter, for pity's sake! "I must tell you that I'm a man of some means."

Oh, bloody hell! She looked even more anxious. Did she think he meant to set her up as he had Annie?

"What I mean," he continued, "is that I intend to once again offer to marry you in a marriage that—while perfectly legal—is not to be a real marriage in the . . . physical sense. This time, I'm not making the offer out of the goodness of my heart but because I wish to ask something of you in return."

Those beautiful blue eyes of her rounded. "I cannot think of what I could possibly offer."

"I wish for you to raise my natural child as if it were your own."

She made not the slightest reaction to what he had proposed. Had she even heard him? "I fear that when I'm dead—as I assure you I will soon be—my father would not honor such an obligation. But obligations to my wife would have the teeth of the law in them. You—and my child—would be well provided for."

"You have no idea how tempted I am to accept. I am, as you know, quite destitute, and I adore children. But this proposition would not be fair to you. I do not share your gloomy premonition. What would happen when you return from war to find yourself saddled with the unsophisticated daughter of a country parson?"

He could not help it. His lazy gaze caressed this vision of loveliness who sat next to him, and he found the prospect of returning to such a woman most welcome. "First, I'm certain I'll not be coming home. And secondly," he peered at her with a wistful longing like nothing he'd ever before experienced, "I believe any man who had a wife like you would count himself blessed."

Her lashes were cast down as a deep blush rose in her cheeks. "Then, sir, I will accept your generous offer."

He'd barely had time to sleep the night before. Because his mother's aunt was married to the Archbishop of Canterbury, he'd rushed off to get the special marriage license directly from Lambeth Palace, stopping first at Rundell & Bridge to purchase a simple gold band for Miss Hensley. After that, he had forced his solicitor to open his office at night in order to draw up the marriage contracts between Miss Elizabeth Hensley and Captain Harold Tate and to make provisions for her and the child in the event of his death.

Then there was the matter of engaging the clergyman to perform the ceremony early in the morning before he had to ride off to Dover. Then he must ensure the witnesses also be at the church at seven in the morning. Kitty would serve as one – after all, she was bringing the babe—and his batman, Morrison, would serve as the other.

Before he had wearily climbed into his bed, he wrote a letter to his parents informing them of his marriage to Elizabeth Hensley, a woman of gentle birth, a woman they need never meet. A pity he could not tell them about the babe.

Not long after daylight intruded into his deep slumber, he realized it was his wedding day, and he sprang from the bed. What a very somber wedding it would be.

An hour later he collected Miss Hensley at the Pulteney Hotel, where he had seen her installed the previous night. His father would have had apoplexy had he known his son was showing up at church on his wedding day in a rented hack!

When she came down the grand stairway at the Pulteney, his mouth went dry and he almost lost his breath. In her pale blue dress that was trimmed in white lace, she looked more like a girl coming out at her first ball than a woman about to become an officer's wife. She was without a doubt the loveliest creature he'd ever seen. Had the young men back in her village of Upper Frampington—wherever in the hell that was—been completely blind? It was incredible that she had not been snatched up within a week of leaving the schoolroom.

And it was understandable how the vile man who had been her employer could have wished to bed her. Curse the damned man!

After they got in the hackney he turned and addressed her. "It has suddenly occurred to me how little I know of you, Miss Hensley. How old are you?"

"I will be twenty next month."

He nodded. "I hope you slept well."

"Of course I didn't sleep well! My mind was entirely too occupied. How about you? Did you sleep well?"

"I slept like a dead man—once I accomplished all I needed to do. My solicitor will call on you later today at the Pulteney and apprise you of the financial matters. There should be enough for you to live modestly but comfortably. My solicitor will help you in any way you desire."

"Do you have any family who will attend this morning's ceremony?"

"No. They are all in Derbyshire. I have this morning dispatched a letter to them apprising them of the marriage."

She nodded somberly.

"I'm afraid I shall have to fly as soon as the service is completed," he said.

"You will give me your direction so that I can write to you?"

He could not allow her to do so. It would only make it harder on both of them. Because of the certainty of his death. "It's best that you don't."

Her face was incredibly sad. "You must tell me about the child."

He harrumphed. "I know so little. I only learned of her existence yesterday, though I have no doubts about her paternity. She is six months of age. I left England fifteen months ago and have continued to make provisions for the child's mother."

"You were not married to her?"

He did not respond for a moment. "She was not the sort of woman one asks to become a wife." He hated like the devil having to make such an admissions to an innocent like Miss Hensley. He could not even look her in the face. No doubt, she was blushing.

"I see."

He would wager Annie's sort of woman had never inhabited Upper Frampington.

"What is the babe's name?"

"The woman who has been caring for her calls her Fanny. She saw that she was baptized after the babe's mother died in childbed. The child's name was recorded as Frances Davis."

The hackney pulled up at St. Clement's, and he turned to her, taking her gloved hands in his. "I won't be able to speak to you privately after the ceremony. I wish you—and Fanny—well."

"And I will pray for you."

Chapter 1

London, Two years later

"I'm a viscountess?" In her entire one and twenty years Elizabeth had never been more astonished. She could not remove her gaze from the aging solicitor who sat across the desk from her perusing documents. Was the poor man delusional? "Surely, Mr. Ferguson, you have mistaken me for another of your clients."

"I think not, Mrs. Tate. You are married to Harold Tate, who has ascended to the Broxbourne viscountancy upon the recent death of his father. It is likely your husband has not yet learned of his elevation, owing to the difficulty of communication to the Peninsula."

Just hearing Harry's name and learning he was still alive allowed her to relax. She had been tied in knots since receiving the summons to Mr. Ferguson's establishment. With each churn of the carriage wheels coming here, she had feared the solicitor was going to tell her that her husband had died.

And now she was a viscountess! "You are absolutely certain?"

"Absolutely. I've been retained by Lord Broxbourne's family for more than forty years."

She would love to have quizzed him about the family. She knew nothing about any of them. To query the solicitor, though, would indicate what a hideous sham this marriage was, and Elizabeth was far too proud to reveal the desperation that made her wed him.

Mr. Ferguson cleared his throat. "I also am in possession of a letter to you from the dowager viscountess. She says she will be delighted to have you for Christmas and is looking forward to showing you your new home."

Elizabeth's heart began to beat prodigiously rapidly. How terribly awkward that would be! She was, after all, an imposter. "Is the dowager not mired in melancholy after her grievous loss so very recently?"

"Because Lord Broxbourne had been gravely ill for several weeks, his viscountess—a most religious woman—imparted to me that her husband's passing was a blessing. It is her belief that he's in a better place."

The way Mr. Ferguson phrased the last indicated to Elizabeth he was a nonbeliever. She was very sorry for him.

He handed her the letter from her mother-in-law but continued to talk. "It is also my pleasure to tell you your income is going to increase dramatically. For the present, you can expect to have at your disposal at least four times what you have now, but as Farley Manor is a much larger home with many more servants than you are accustomed to, the larger income is necessary. It will be up to the new Lord Broxbourne to determine the exact settlements upon each family member. "

Each family member? How many were there? How Elizabeth longed to question Mr. Ferguson, but she was too embarrassed to admit her total dearth of knowledge about the man she had married two years ago and never heard from since.

"The dowager has asked for your direction as she plans to send the Broxbourne carriage to take you to Farley Manor on Wednesday."

Wednesday? That was a mere two days off! Oh, dear, what was she to do? She couldn't go. She would feel the most mercenary usurper on God's planet. And Harry's family would be sure to learn immediately that she was not *really* his wife.

"Would it be possible, do you think, Mr. Ferguson, for me to decline the title and let the dowager continue to preside over Farley Hall? I'm in no way qualified to take her place."

He shook his head. "The Broxbourne's are a very old family mired in traditions going back for hundreds of years. It is not *your* prerogative to decline such an honor, and you would discredit your husband by even attempting to do something so unconventional. Besides, the dowager has already moved out of the viscountess's chambers and had them made ready for you."

She stiffened. *What about Fanny?* "Does Lady Broxbourne know of my . . .husband's child?" She had started to call Fanny her own child for that is exactly how she thought of the precious little girl who'd enriched her own life so immeasurably.

He cleared his throat. "I do not believe she does."

"It is really best that I not go to Farley Manor because I go nowhere without the child. Furthermore, I should die if Harry's family should shun her in any way." Why had she called him Harry? She had always thought of him as Harry, but it was far too intimate, especially to use with his solicitor.

The silver-haired man eyed her, his bushy brows lowered. "I cannot advise you. I told you what your duty is. You must know what your husband's thoughts are about revealing the child's paternity?"

How could she tell this man she not only did not know of her husband's thoughts about anything, she had not even communicated with him in two years?

In any decision regarding Fanny, Elizabeth would defer to no one. She alone knew what was best for *her* child.

The solicitor watched Elizabeth, obviously waiting for a response she was incapable of giving. "I would suggest, Mrs. Tate, you ask yourself what would your husband want you to do. Lord Broxbourne has always been possessed of a keen sense of duty."

Although she had been in her husband's presence for less than two hours, she had quickly surmised that he was guided by an acute sense of duty.

As she thought of him, she knew what she must do. Not for her. For her child. Harry would want his child acknowledged. He would want Fanny to come to Farley Manor now that his stern father was not there.

For the man she had married was an honorable man.

Night had already come to the Derbyshire hill country by the time Elizabeth and Fanny neared Farley Manor. Night came much earlier this time of year, and nights were so much darker here in the country away from the busy Capital. She peered from the window as the coach turned from the main road. Everything looked black and white. White snow against black sky.

"Are we there yet, Mama?" Fanny asked.

Elizabeth smiled as she looked down at Fanny's dark little head barely poking above the rug mother and daughter shared. The child must have asked the question a hundred times. Because the carriage was speeding toward a stately home in the distance as steadily as a compass points north, Elizabeth felt she could finally give the little girl an affirmative answer. "I believe we're very close, my sweet."

Moonlight illuminated the very large house. Its irregular roofline with at least twenty chimneys poking from it indicated the house had likely been constructed over several generations. It did not seem to belong to a single era. It was neither Tudor nor influenced by the current passion for Palladian. It was just a large English country home.

Her pulse accelerated. It would now be her home. And Fanny's. She hugged the child to her.

"I'm cold," Fanny said.

"I know, love. We'll soon be in a warm house."

Despite the twenty chimneys, Elizabeth feared the house would be big and drafty and exceedingly cold.

She prayed their welcome would not be so.

By the time Elizabeth and Fanny reached the front door, it swept open. A man of middle age and formal demeanor greeted them, his gaze flicking from mother to daughter. "Lady Broxbourne?"

Lady Broxbourne? So unaccustomed was she

to even the notion of being referred to in such a manner, Elizabeth was confused. Before she had the opportunity to embarrass herself further, she realized he was addressing her. "Yes."

"Come right in. The family is expecting you."

Once inside, she and Fanny divested themselves of their damp cloaks.

She had been right about the drafty rooms. It was beastly cold as they followed him along cold stone floors beneath soaring ceilings. She continued to keep her hands encased in her fur muff.

They had entered into a rather square corridor from which one could ascend a broad stone stairway anchored by a pair of chunky Tudor newel posts where banisters of age-darkened oak terminated. Huge paintings of Elizabethan-looking men and women stared down at them from walls papered in a floral print as they passed several doorways.

Elizabeth could only imagine what was going through the little girl's mind as she clutched her hand tightly. She had never been in so large a house before, but for that matter, neither had Elizabeth! And while Fanny might be apprehensive over these strange new surroundings, the dear child could not be more terrified than her mother. Elizabeth felt as if tin cups clanged against the walls of her heaving chest.

The butler led them to a vast chamber that Elizabeth presumed was the drawing room. He stopped in the room's doorway and announced her. Gripping Fanny's hand even more tightly—as if to draw strength from the tiny child—Elizabeth entered the chamber, forcing a smile.

Her gaze fanned over the room which was softened by Turkey carpets and warmed by a fireplace at either end of the chamber. Though the room was large, it had an intimate feel.

Would that the expressions of the faces of those assembled were as comforting.

She immediately knew the fair pretty woman who could not possibly be fifty had to be Harry's mother, not because they resembled in any way but because she was the only person of the five others in the chamber who was over thirty years of age. Another woman looked exceedingly like Harry and also seemed to be the same age as he. The man seated beside her—the only man present, other than the butler—also looked the same age. She surmised he must be married to the woman who looked so much like Harry. Two other, younger women were seated at a game table where they'd been playing chess.

The young man with curly blond hair spoke first. "By Jove! Knew when Harry shackled himself it would be to a pretty blonde." He had done Elizabeth the goodness of standing when she entered the chamber.

"Robert!" The woman Elizabeth presumed to be his wife turned a scolding countenance upon him. "You'll embarrass the poor lady." She raised herself to her considerable height and came forward, curtseying. "Allow me to introduce myself. I am Harry's eldest sister, Susan, and I should like to present you to our mother." She indicated the lovely older woman.

Elizabeth curtsied. "A pleasure to meet you, my lady."

A tight smile barely moved the woman's mouth as her gaze fell on Fanny. Uncomfortable with strangers, the little girl buried her face in her mother's skirts.

"It is a pleasure to finally make your acquaintance," the dowager said. Her gaze shifted to Fanny as Elizabeth picked up the child in an effort to comfort her. "And who is the lovely little girl?"

No one could look at Fanny and not see her father. Her mahogany hair was his hair. Her piercing black eyes were his eyes. Even the tiny cleft in her chin was his. But Elizabeth did not know how Harry would want Fanny introduced. She could hardly take the liberty to announce to her husband's family that this beautiful child was his bastard. "This is my daughter, Fanny," Elizabeth said after an awkward pause.

The dowager carefully masked her emotions. "I have not been told about the child." She softened her voice and asked Fanny, "Pray, child, how old are you?"

Her little hands digging into Elizabeth, she said, "Two half."

Elizabeth could tell the dowager was doing the arithmetic. She would, of course, realize the babe was born out of wedlock. Lady Broxbourne's face went from quizzing, to icy, then—as would a well-brought-up lady—she recovered and said to Fanny, "You will have a cousin very close to your own age to play with."

"What's a cousin?" Fanny asked, peering up at Elizabeth.

"It's something like a sister."

"Brother is more like it," Susan said. "It appears Mama suddenly finds herself grandmother to three. I have two sons, but Fanny will be the first granddaughter."

"How old are your lads?" Elizabeth asked.

"Our Robbie is six, and Tommy is three and a half."

Elizabeth was delighted that Fanny would finally have the opportunity to play with other children.

Susan linked her arm to Elizabeth's. "Let me make you known to my husband, Robert Townshend, and my sisters."

The young women who had been playing chess had directed their full attention to Elizabeth.

"The blonde who resembles Mama is Diana, and the one who resembles Harry and me is Sarah."

As the younger sisters stood, Elizabeth became ever more acutely aware of how out of place she was here. These ladies' dresses looked as if they had been copied from Ackerman's newest magazine. Elizabeth spent little on clothing, even though Harry gave her a generous allowance. Why would she need fine clothes? She never entered Society. The two dresses she possessed she had sewn herself. And they looked it.

"I'm ever so happy to meet you, Sister," Diana said, curtsying.

"I feel the very same," the other sister said. "I declare, you and I must be the same age."

"I am one and twenty," Elizabeth said.

"And I but one year elder—much closer in age to you than I am to my other sisters," Sarah said.

The sisters at least were excessively gracious. "As an only child, I am delighted to finally have a family."

Taking Elizabeth with her, Susan returned to the silken sofa she had been sharing with Robert.

"I confess I'm astonished at the strong resemblance between you and Harry," Elizabeth said. She had slipped and called him Harry again. "And Sarah, too." Would they comment on how strongly Fanny resembled her father?

"They all resemble my late husband," the dowager said, bowing her head. "God rest his dear soul." Her gaze settled on her youngest child. "Only my baby looks like me."

Elizabeth found it odd that none of them commented on Fanny, who sat on her lap, thumb shoved in her mouth as she looked around at what was likely the largest room she had ever been in.

"Would you like to have the nurse collect Fanny?" Lady Broxbourne asked.

Elizabeth hugged the child tighter. "Not this first night. She's a bit frightened by the unfamiliar setting and people she doesn't know. I'll keep her with me."

There was a flicker of kindness in the older woman's gaze.

"Harry—I need to remember that he will now be called Broxbourne—wrote that you're the daughter of clergyman," the dowager said.

She could not help but wonder what else Harry had told his family about her. "Yes. I lost my papa three years ago."

"And your mother?" the dowager asked.

"She died when I was eight."

The dowager's brows lowered. "Have you no family?"

"It has been just Fanny and me."

"I, for one, will be happy we won't have to share you with any other family," Sarah said.

"That is very kind of you." Elizabeth's gaze

went from Sarah to Susan. "Do you live at Farley Manor?"

"No. We're in Lincolnshire, but we come back to Farley for Christmas every year. It's such a wonderful place for the children."

"She dare not stay away from Farley too long because it's a severe deprivation for this grandmother not to be able to see my precious little lads," the dowager said.

So the woman was not as icy as her stiff blond demeanor at first suggested. Elizabeth wondered if she would ever feel such deep affection for her precious Fanny.

"Tell me," Elizabeth said, addressing Harry's mother, "has my husband learned of his father's passing?"

The older woman shrugged."I wrote the letter myself, but sometimes it's months before letters reach him."

"I asked Palmerston to see what he could do to ensure the letter was delivered to Harry, er, Broxbourne, as speedily as possible," Robert said.

"The Secretary of War?" Elizabeth asked.

He nodded.

"Robert's a member of the House of Commons," Susan explained.

Elizabeth had never met an M.P. before. Whatever had possessed her to come here? She wasn't of their world and did not belong here. It wasn't as if she really was Harry's wife. "Then I am most honored to meet you."

"As we're all happy to meet you," Susan said.

They would not think so if they knew the truth.

"We should have made the effort to make your acquaintance sooner, but my husband's grave state of health for so very long prevented me from doing so."

"I understand," Elizabeth said. "Was your husband a great deal older than you? I must own, you are much younger than I expected."

The dowager offered her another tight smile. "My dear husband and I were separated by the same number of years as you and Harry."

Which was? Elizabeth had no idea how old Harry was, but she could not reveal how little she knew about him. She started to ask Susan her age, but she was so close in age and appearance to her brother, Elizabeth feared they might be twins, and if they were, his real wife would know such a thing. Of course, Susan had introduced herself as Harry's *eldest* sister. Did that mean eldest of all three sisters? Or did it mean she was older than Harry?

Perhaps there was a less obvious way to introduce the topic. Elizabeth turned to Susan. "Forgive me my ignorance, but which of you is eldest, you or Harry?" Even if they were twins, a twin always claimed to know which one drew breath first.

"Me," Susan answered. "I'm eight and twenty—a year almost to the day older than Harry."

The two younger sisters had come to sit upon the sofa near their mother. "My lady," Diana said to Elizabeth, making Elizabeth feel excessively awkward, "how did you meet Harry? Was it at Almack's?"

Even though Elizabeth was not of the *ton*, she knew about London's Almack's assembly rooms where only the cream of Society gained entrance. She shook her head. "I did not mingle in such high levels of Society. My father was a poor country parson."

"Then however did you meet my son?"

What was she to say? She could hardly tell them the truth. But, she suddenly realized, she could give them *some* of the truth. "We met at church."

Robert's mouth gaped open in astonishment. "Harry at church?"

Sarah eyed her with disbelief. "I cannot imagine my brother attending church in London when there are so many other claims on one's interest."

"That certainly doesn't sound like the Harry I know from Oxford," Robert said.

"I believe you all malign him," Elizabeth said good naturedly. "He seemed very close to God the day I met him, and I don't mean to alarm any of you, but he was most melancholy over returning to the Peninsula." Because it would be too distressful to his family, she could not reveal more, could not tell them he expected to die. She ought to change the subject. She turned back to face Susan. "Pray, how did you and Mr. Townshend meet?"

"I'm surprised Harry didn't tell you. You see, Robert and Harry have been best friends ever since Eton. I fell madly in love with Robert when I was thirteen, but it took him much longer." She gazed lovingly into her husband's good-natured face.

Robert kissed her cheek, then met Elizabeth's gaze. "I thought it odd to learn of Harry's marriage. We were not accustomed to keeping things from one another."

Elizabeth could tell he was suspicious, but before she could comment, a great commotion arose. Dogs began to bark, and the butler was making exclamations.

The door to the drawing room burst open, and there stood the new Viscount Broxbourne.

CHAPTER 2

It was not his much-loved mother or his dear sisters or even good old Townshend who captured his attention as he stood in the drawing room's doorway, shaking the snow from his cap and handing it to Collins. He had almost forgotten about the beautiful young woman he had so hastily married. Until he saw her sitting in his family circle, even more lovely than he remembered. His gaze shifted to the little girl on her lap. Could that child who so strongly resembled Susan be Fanny? His child? A lump the size of an egg seemed lodged in his chest.

All of those he loved most in the world were in this very room where he had spent so much of his life. He had never thought to see any of them again, never thought he would ever again set foot inside this chamber's comforting walls. He was almost overcome with emotions.

His sisters flew toward him, exclamations bellowing, arms encircling. Even his demure mother had tossed down her embroidery and presented her sweet face for his obligatory peck on her cheek.

As happy as he was to see them, his thoughts were on Elizabeth. How would he greet her? How much of the truth had she told his family?

A flurry of questions and professions of excitement came so rapidly, it was impossible to respond to any. He was aware that Townshend had come to slap him on the back. "Where are your regimentals, old fellow?"

Finally he'd been able to isolate one question to respond to. "I've sold my colors."

"Oh, my darling," his mother said, "I am so very happy you'll not be going back."

He put his arm around her. "Now that Papa's gone, it's my duty to run Farley and . . . " His gaze shifted to his two youngest sisters. . ."see that Sarah and Diana find husbands."

Diana began to giggle. "Then I am decidedly happy you've come home, Harry."

"Gotta call him Broxbourne now," Townshend said.

His wife—the only person in the chamber still seated—had not removed her gaze from him, and even though he managed to communicate with his family, she commanded his attention in the same way as a dazzling sunset in the western sky.

"Now ladies," Townshend said in his booming voice, "allow the poor man to hug his wife. He hasn't seen her in these two years past."

Harry's eyes locked with hers. A tentative smile lifted the corners of her mouth. She had the look of an angel about her with her flaxen locks and ivory skin and the radiance that seemed to surround her. His gaze trailed from her beautiful face to the blue velvet dress she wore. She stood up the child, then stood herself. "How wonderful to see you home safely," she said.

He moved to her, arms outstretched. "My dear wife, how very good it is to see you."

She fell into his embrace and clasped her arms tightly around him. "Oh, my lord, I've prayed so fervently that you would return!"

Damn, but she felt good in his arms! He hadn't

realized how tiny she was. He did not want to release her, but he could feel a decided tug upon her as the little girl affixed herself to her. He pulled back and peered at the child. "This cannot be Fanny?"

The lovely little girl looked up at him, nodding. "I am, too, Fanny."

He lowered himself to her level. "Would you allow me to pick you up?"

The quizzing gaze of her dark eyes went from him to Elizabeth.

"Let him pick you up, love," Elizabeth said.

His heart melted when Fanny lifted those little arms to him. He stood as he drew her to him, astonished at the powerful rush of emotions she elicited in him. His and Elizabeth's eyes locked, and she smiled up at them, her hand resting gently on his sleeve. Life was good!

He wished to hell he knew what she had told his family about Fanny. The three of them sat together on the sofa across from where his mother had taken her seat.

"Your wife just arrived minutes before you," his mother told him.

His glance whisked to Elizabeth's.

"I was just getting acquainted with your family, my lord," she said.

How clever of her to anticipate his questions.

"And as delighted as we all are to have you home, Broxbourne, I know you and your wife are weary from your journeys." Leave it to his pragmatic mother to be the first to address him by the name of her beloved husband. It was as if she were encouraging him to fill the very deep void left by the gregarious man who had been his father.

Grief over his father's loss flickered anew now that he was once again in the room he so associated with his parents, but there was too much joy here now to dwell on such low thoughts. He must put the darkness behind him now that he was back at Farley Manor. "I do believe I could sleep for a week. I haven't really slept in four days."

"I will have dinner sent to you and her ladyship," his mother said. "Your possessions were, of course, moved to the viscount's chambers. I've had it redone with the same colors as your former room."

He nodded to her, glad to be able to quiz his wife before being subjected to questions from his family. "Of course, you will have eaten hours ago, if you still keep the same hours as you always did."

Robert answered. "How well you know your mother. She is most inflexible."

"Now, Robert," Susan countered, "that's not so. Mama has been most accommodating. She insisted on vacating the viscountess's chambers the very week of Papa's passing."

So Elizabeth's chambers would adjoin his. How. . . interesting. At least they would be able to make sure they were on the same page in their dealings with his family. He faced his . . . his wife. "Come with me, my dear. I know you must be fatigued."

"Indeed I am."

He peered down at Fanny's dark hair, wondering what in the blazes he was to do about the child. Would she go to the nursery?

"Fanny's to sleep with me this first night," Elizabeth said.

It was as if she could read his thoughts.

He continued to hold Fanny as they said their farewells to those in the drawing room.

"Tomorrow, my dear son," the dowager said, "you must give your wife the tour of Farley." Then she directed her comments to Elizabeth, "I will be most happy to assist you in any way I can during the transitional period."

Oh dear, Elizabeth thought. The dowager was prepared to turn over the running of Farley Manor to her! How could she extract herself from this whole situation? As she and Harry began to mount that wide staircase in the main corridor, her heartbeat hammered. How grateful she was that he'd been so civil to her when he was bound to think her the most emboldened usurper who ever drew breath. What had ever possessed her to come to Farley Manor? It wasn't as if she belonged in such a grand place. She was embarrassingly ill equipped to oversee such a home.

But then she had never presumed to be a viscountess. She wanted none of the trappings of nobility for herself. But for Fanny she wanted the moon and the stars and all things wonderful. For Fanny *was* of Harry's blood.

Even if the poor little lamb was born on the wrong side of the blanket.

She could not allow herself to look at him. He was far too handsome. For the past two years she had almost convinced herself it had been his dashing uniform with the scarlet coat that made her recall him as an excessively handsome man. But now she knew the uniform had not embellished his good looks. Tonight in the chocolate colored woolens he wore for traveling he was, if possible, even more handsome than he'd been in his regimentals that first day at St. Clement's. And taller, too.

It was also entirely too painful for her to watch him and Fanny together, knowing that he was probably not prepared to claim her as his own child. Even if she did look exactly like him.

Despite that he had behaved toward her with the utmost propriety, he must be excessively angry with her for brazenly showing up at his ancestral home as if she truly belonged there. She could well understand it were he to demand that she flee in the middle of the night in the snow. But how would he explain her to his family?

"So you, too, had just arrived?" he asked her.

With each step she climbed, the trembling which had begun in her chest and reverberated to encompass all of her threatened even her voice. Perhaps she could manage a one-word answer. "Indeed."

"Your first visit?"

"Yes."

They reached the second floor. "You will, of course, have my mother's old chambers."

She felt wretchedly guilty that the dowager had vacated her rooms for her. It wasn't as if she planned on staying. She fully expected Har-, er, the new Lord Broxbourne to throw her out. Even if he was exceedingly kind and up until now the most noble man she had ever encountered.

A man could only sacrifice so much. Now that he was home to England for good, it was only right that he find a wife of his own class, a woman born to become a viscountess, not a country lass like her. It wasn't as if this were a *real* marriage at all. It had never been consummated.

She followed him down a wide corridor lit by wall sconces. They were nearly at the end before he paused at a door and opened it. "Your chambers, my lady." He waved her in.

She wished he would *not* refer to her as *my lady*. She felt far too much the usurper already, and now she could add fraud to her description. What a perfectly dreadful Christmas this was going to be.

The hearth in the chamber was much larger than one would expect in a bedchamber, but then this was a much larger bedchamber than any she had ever before seen. At the opposite end of the room an oil lamp burned beside the huge bed that was draped in purple velvet. The half of the room she stood in must serve as a sitting room. A settee faced the blazing fire, and a lovely writing desk faced a tall window that was also draped in purple velvet.

Fanny stole the words from her mouth. "Oh, it's beautiful!"

Elizabeth met his gaze. "I am very sorry, my lord, I'm the cause of your mother being driven from her chambers."

His features seemed even darker in firelight. "We have much to talk about."

"Then I must first put Fanny to bed." She saw that her valise had already been placed in the room. She opened it and procured a warm night gown for the little girl and instructed her to get ready for bed.

"Then will you tell me a story?" Fanny asked.

"We shall see, love. You must be very quiet for I need to speak to Lord Broxbourne first."

Elizabeth felt incredibly awkward being in a bedchamber with the viscount. She must block from her mind that portion of the room where the bed was. "Please be seated, my lord."

As she came to sit next to him on the settee, her trembling increased, but her determination to resolve this embarrassing situation overrode any personal embarrassment. "I shouldn't have come," she began. "I assure you I have no desire to be a viscountess. My only motivation in coming here was Fanny."

He nodded thoughtfully, his pensive face otherwise inscrutable. "What exactly did you tell my family about her?" He had lowered his voice so the child could not hear them discussing her.

"I did not know what you wanted to say about her, so I told them she was my child—which is how I feel about her. Unfortunately, your mother asked her how old she is, and Fanny was quick to tell her she was two and a half." She put index finger to her lips, got up and tiptoed toward the bed. Fanny was already fast asleep.

"Is she asleep?" he asked.

She nodded.

"So my mother knows Fanny was born before our wedding." He spoke in a soft voice, almost as if he were thinking aloud.

"No doubt, she thinks I'm a tart."

He chuckled. "My dear lady, I cannot believe anyone would think you a tart."

"One thing is for sure. They all must know she's yours. Did you notice how remarkably she resembles you?"

He nodded. "But fortunately, she's pretty."

"And she's ever so clever and a perfect angel."

"Spoken like a true mother."

"Which is exactly how I think of myself, and I warn you, my lord, I would put up the most tremendous fight the mighty Tate family has ever seen if one of you tries to take her away from me." That is why Elizabeth spent very little of the allowance Harry had provided for her. She feared she would need the money one day to procure legal services if the Tates ever tried to remove Fanny from her.

"Whoa!" He held up a palm. "I would be a most heartless creature were I to separate the poor child from her mother."

Elizabeth's shoulders sagged with relief. "I tried to explain to your solicitor that I did not want to come to Farley Manor, that I had no intentions of becoming the Viscountess Broxbourne, but he insisted. I have never been more astonished in my life than I was three days ago when I learned that you were the son of a viscount."

"Sorry. I suppose I should have told you a bit more about myself."

"Of course, neither of us believed we would ever meet again, and I never imagined I'd ever meet your family."

"And here you are!"

"What are we going to do? You must, of course, see to annulling the marriage."

His brows lowered. "Annul a holy sacrament?"

"I will own, I don't like the idea, but I'm hardly qualified to be a viscountess. You must be allowed to exercise your own free choice and select a proper lady to become Lady Broxbourne."

Those black eyes of his sparkled. "Do not disparage yourself. You are a proper lady."

"I am in no way qualified to serve as your viscountess. Do you realize this bedchamber is likely larger than the entire house in which I grew up?"

He shrugged. "So?"

"And look at the way I am dressed! I felt incredibly inferior next to your lovely sisters."

"That's ridiculous! As much as I love my sisters, I instantly perceived that you were the prettiest lady in the room."

Oh dear. She could feel the blush climbing into her cheeks. "I assure you, I looked exceedingly dowdy next to the impeccably dressed Tate family."

He touched the blue velvet of her sleeve and spoke in a husky voice. "This dress is lovely, but if you don't think it smart enough you are at liberty to remedy any wardrobe deficiencies. I assure you my unwed sisters have no qualms about spending Tate funds on their attire."

"That is not what I meant. You have been most generous already to me. If I chose to dress as a fine lady, I could. But I am not a fine lady."

Anger flashed across his face. "You malign the mother of my child."

She couldn't help it. She had to smile. "You are behaving most gallantly, my lord, but I cannot allow you to throw away your future happiness by accepting a wife from such humble origins." Oh, dear. Had he been terribly in love with Fanny's mother? Had he decided he would never love again? Is that why he could throw away his future with the likes of her?

He was a young man. He would find love again—with a woman who was of the *ton*, a woman who belonged at Farley Manor. "If only I hadn't come. You could have told your family I died, and you could have quietly annulled the marriage, then married a woman your family would be happy to accept as Lady Broxbourne."

"Yes, it would have simplified matters if you hadn't come."

"Then I will leave tonight."

Chapter 3

The clergyman's daughter most decidedly had a mind of her own. "You will not leave Farley in the middle of a snow storm!" he said. "At least, not with *my* daughter."

Those beautiful blue eyes of hers narrowed. "How dare you use that child in such a way!"

"I have as much to say about her welfare as you do. Would you endanger her in that manner?"

The rigidity in her shoulders collapsed. "No, I don't suppose I could. And I wouldn't leave without her, either. But I am most willing to leave at the earliest opportunity."

"I think not."

"Why?"

"It just won't do. Don't you see, you're a proper lady, and it will appear that I've compromised you. I can't live with such a stain."

"It's not as if anyone who knows you knows me."

"Nevertheless, you're not the sort of woman whose reputation one ruins." He got to his feet. "And now, madam, I shall go to my room to sleep." He started toward a door next to the chimney piece.

She leapt to her feet, thrusting hands to waist. "Where do you think you're going?"

"The adjoining chamber happens to be my room!"

She stomped her foot. "You can't go yet. We

must decide what we're going to tell your family tomorrow."

He glared at the maddening woman. "Tomorrow, madam, you will pretend to be my devoted wife."

Her mouth formed a perfect O as she angrily watched him storm from her chamber.

He wasn't sure how the capable staff had managed it, but his chamber was already warm from the blazing wood fire in the hearth, and fresh linens had been put on his bed. Damn but he was tired. It seemed almost incomprehensible that four days ago he'd been in Portugal and now here he was back at Farley Manor surrounded by all those he loved. Save his dear Papa, whom he gravely missed.

Having little Fanny here gave him a measure of happiness. It was right that upon his father's passing, the Tate blood would continue to flow into another generation. God, but the child was exquisite! How could he not acknowledge her? Of course, he would have to wait a bit. There were too many changes too fast at Farley.

Poor Mama was only now adjusting to Christmas without her mate. He liked to think she was happy to have her only son back home. He'd known as soon as he received her letter that he must return to Farley. Though her letter was full of bravado about Papa being in a better place and how she was managing very nicely in the dowager's wing without him, Harry could read between the lines. She needed him. And his unwed sisters needed him.

And, damn, but he was happy to be home.

Whether she knew it or not, Elizabeth needed him. As did the child.

It hurt him that there was nothing he could do to legitimize his natural child. He vowed to acknowledge her at the earliest opportunity, not publicly because illegitimacy could stain the poor creature, but she would be known as his beloved ward, with only those in his family knowing the full truth.

But should he allow his family—and even little Fanny herself—to think Elizabeth had given birth to her out of wedlock? He felt guilty that Elizabeth was being held culpable for sins he had committed. There was the fact, though, that she wished to claim Fanny as her own. What in the devil was best?

He extinguished the light and climbed beneath the covers of his bed that was draped in claret velvet. He could not remember the last time he had actually slept in a real bed. God, it felt good. As fatigued as he was, though, he was too keyed up to sleep. He was astonished that he'd nearly forgotten about Elizabeth's existence until he saw her in the drawing room of Farley Manor tonight. She looked as if she belonged there every bit as much as his sisters.

The very sight of her had awakened desires he had long denied. When he had stood at the doorway and gazed at Elizabeth's fair blond beauty as she hugged his precious child on her lap, powerful emotions had nearly swamped him.

And the child? She had completely captured his heart the moment she lifted those little arms to him.

It would take no effort on Elizabeth's part for him to become besotted over the beauty.

He recalled how profoundly he had been affected by her on the day of their wedding. Try as he might, he'd been unable to purge the vision of her loveliness as she stood at the altar beside him, plighting her life to his before God and man. During his beastly journey back to the Peninsula, her loveliness was emblazoned upon his memory in the same indestructible way a silversmith etches his mark on a fine sterling tray.

He had never allowed himself to dream of what it would have been like to truly be married to an angel like her. It would have been too painful to contemplate.

He was still stunned that his life had been spared, still reveling in the realization that he was back at Farley Manor for good. This was the one place in all the world where he wanted to be.

He was now seven and twenty and had seen far more of the world than he cared to see. It was time to settle. And despite what Elizabeth thought, he meant to settle with her.

He could comb the world over and never find a woman he would prefer over her. Her appeal went far deeper than her incredible beauty. Even though he'd not been with her very much, he knew the goodness of her heart, especially to his lovely little girl.

By Jove! He was going to make Elizabeth fall in love with him.

He was already half in love with her. By Christmas, this would be a real marriage.

Which he suddenly realized was what he wanted more than anything.

She did not belong here. Truly she didn't. Why, then, did this bedchamber envelop her like Grandma's counterpane? She lay within the peace of the big bed so high off the ground, she'd had to climb steps to it. Fanny's warm little body beside hers and the velvet curtains trapping the warmth into their little square gave her a feeling of safety unlike anything she had experienced since her father had died.

Of course, she had to leave Farley Manor. Lord Broxbourne had been all that was gallant both that first day and again tonight, but she could not allow him to throw away all prospect of happiness. He deserved a fine wife of his own class. He deserved a wife who won his mother's approval. He deserved a wife who loved him as mightily as Elizabeth loved Fanny.

But what woman would not fall in love with him? Even were he not so handsome, and were he not titled, and were he not rich, any woman would fall in love with a man possessed of such an unwavering sense of honor.

How would she manage to extract herself from this situation?

She could only barely tell the sun had risen through a slight gap in the velvet drapes which encased their bed, so it was not the light that had awakened her. It was a trembling upon her mattress. What in the world? She rolled over, and discovered Fanny jumping upon the bed as if she were a circus performer! "Young lady! You will stop that right now."

"Why?" She continued bobbing up and down.

Elizabeth sat up. "Because you might hurt yourself." She hauled the tiny child into her arms and gave her several smacking kisses. "I love you, silly goose."

"I love you."

"Let's get dressed and go meet your cousins!"

Embarrassingly, Elizabeth put on the same blue velvet she'd worn the night before. She only possessed two dresses, and she would save the best for the dinner table. She knew the nobility always dressed for dinner.

Once they were dressed, she was in a quandary as to where to go. The house was so large. Perhaps she would ask the viscount. She tentatively walked to the connecting door and knocked.

"You may come in, Lady Broxbourne." The beastly man persisted in calling her by that name she was so woefully qualified to take. Why could his mother not continue being the mistress of Farley Manor?

Holding Fanny's hand, she walked into a scarlet chamber filled with morning sun from a half a dozen tall casements, and there in the middle of the bed sat the viscount, his chest bare. In her entire life, Elizabeth had never seen a man without a shirt. Her modest father had not thought it proper to even be seen without his coat. She gasped, and clasped her hand to her eyes.

"My dear wife," he exclaimed, "there is nothing improper in seeing one's husband without a shirt."

She removed her hand from her face and glared at him. Her mouth went dry. He was the most provocative looking man she had ever beheld. And he was magnificent. Any sculptor would count himself blessed to have such a manly model. For a few seconds, she lost her train of thought, then she gathered her wits. "But you aren't really my husband!"

"I most certainly am. I had the settlements

appropriately drawn up by my highly qualified solicitor, and did I not say my vows to you—in front of witnesses, mind you—at St. Clement's Church?"

Her hands went to her hips. "You know very well what I mean."

His gaze shifted to Fanny, and his teasing manner vanished. "Pray, wife, hand me a shirt."

She walked to the linen press and found a shirt of ivory linen and took it to him. That is when it suddenly occurred to her that he wore nothing at all. Thankfully, his coverings concealed the lower half of his body.

He shrugged into the shirt, then directed his full attention to Fanny. "Hello, Fanny."

"Hello."

"I am going to take you to meet your cousins this morning. Tommy is rather close to your size."

"Is Tommy a sister?" she asked in her whispery little child's voice.

Elizabeth was so proud of her. It seemed incredible that just months ago she'd been a baby, and now she was able to converse with adults. At least as well as a child of two and half could.

"Have you eaten yet?" he asked Elizabeth.

"No, sir. That is one reason I elected to disturb you this morning."

"You're not disturbing me."

"I do not know where to go. You must own, Farley Manor is a very large house."

"Give me ten minutes to dress and shave, then I'll take you to breakfast myself."

"This first morning," he told Elizabeth before showing her and his sweet little daughter to the sunny morning room, "we will allow Fanny to eat with us. Pray, don't let my mother know. She is very strict about children taking meals in the nursery." He lowered himself to the beautiful child. "Will you allow me to carry you?"

A smile lighted her little face as she nodded.

He could scarcely believe he was now master of Farley Manor. Even though, as the only son, he'd always known he was in line to inherit, he had believed he would die on an Iberian battlefield. That was one reason he'd not hesitated to marry Elizabeth. Her widow's portion would have come out of the entailment due to go to a distant cousin he'd never met.

They each helped themselves to cups of tea from the sideboard, and Elizabeth poured some milk into a cup for Fanny. She put two pieces of toast on a plate and scooped marmalade onto it before sitting down at the big mahogany table.

"And what, my little miss, do you want?" he asked Fanny, still holding her.

"Toast and that." Fanny pointed to the grape jelly.

When he reached the table, he set Fanny on his lap. "She's much too little for such a big table," he told Elizabeth.

"I'm actually quite astonished she's allowing you to carry her about," Elizabeth said. "She's usually leery of strangers."

How deeply it hurt to think he was a stranger to his own child. "I intend to remedy that."

"You really must watch her with that grape jelly. It will be all over her pretty dress."

He took a damask napkin and tied it around her neck. "Eat to your heart's content, little one."

He had to laugh. By the time she had finished

attacking the toast, her face was dabbled with bright purple. He and Elizabeth exchanged amused smiles.

"I begin to understand why your mother might not want little ones at her fine table."

"It is now *your* table, my lady. Besides, the table in the nursery is much more her size."

When they finished, they took Fanny to the nursery, but his nephews weren't there. "I'll check in Susan's chamber. Come along," he said.

His sister was still in bed, with a son snuggled on either side of her. "Oh Har-, Broxbourne, you will finally meet my lads."

"Don't tell me," he said, winking at the sister who was closest to him in age. "The lad with the dark hair is Robbie, and the blond is Tommy."

Each of the boys nodded.

Susan beamed proudly. "This, boys is your uncle."

"The captain?" Robbie asked, his eyes flashing with excitement.

"Not anymore," Harry said. "I'm back to Farley for good. And I've brought you lads a soldierly present."

Their eyes rounded with excitement.

"I am told the epaulets off dead French soldiers are much prized," he muttered, "so I brought home a pair for my nephews."

"How lovely of you," Susan said.

Still holding Fanny—he rather liked the feel of the dear child—he eyed his nephews. "I declare," he said, peering at Tommy, "you're a fine looking lad, even if you do look exactly like your father."

"And Robbie looks exactly like his uncle Broxbourne," Susan said, her gaze shifting to Fanny. There was no way he could ever deny

Fanny's paternity.

Harry smiled. "Lucky lad."

Robbie began to giggle.

Just then Robert entered the chamber. Unlike his wife, he was fully dressed. "Oh, there you are, Broxbourne. Fancy a ride?"

"Not this morning. I'm pledged to give my wife the tour or Farley."

"I was going to take the lads to the mews. They're mad over horses. Go get your coats."

"You must take Fanny," Susan said. I'm sure she'd love to see the new foal, and she can play with Tommy, too."

His little daughter had not been able to remove her eyes from the lads. He suspected she had not had the opportunity to be around other children.

Elizabeth came closer to her. "You can go with these little boys to see a baby horse."

Tommy has scooted off the bed and came up to them. Harry stood Fanny up beside the three-year-old lad. The top of her dark head was level with his nose. Both of them were fascinated with each other.

"Take the little girl's hand, love," Susan said in a sweet voice.

The little fellow took her hand, and to Harry's astonishment, she was perfectly comfortable walking away with her cousin. He faced Elizabeth, and they both shrugged.

Elizabeth went scurrying after her. "Allow me to fetch her coat and gloves."

"I must claim Lady Broxbourne this afternoon," Susan said.

Harry nodded. "I will need to meet with Hinckley."

After the children happily went off with Robert,

Harry proffered his arm to his wife. They went back down the broad staircase beneath huge crystal chandeliers, and when they reached the entry hall, he stopped. "Farley is not grand by English country house standards. It's just a large family home that's evolved over the last three hundred years." He pointed to a huge painting of a man garbed in tights and plumed hat. "That was the first viscount. He's the one who originally built Farley Manor, but it's been modified and enlarged several times since." For the life of him, he failed to see any resemblance between that first earl and any of his present offspring.

From that broad, stone floored corridor, several tall carved wood doors opened. One was to the library. "This is one of my favorite rooms," he told her as they entered the chamber. The Tate family had always taken pride in their hand-tooled leather books, and he especially liked the way the library had been laid out with reading nooks arranged around the tall casement windows above cushioned window seats.

"It's such a comforting room," she said, her gaze spanning the dark wood cases on either side of the hearth, where a fire had been laid. "One of the saddest days of my life was when I had to sell Papa's library because I had nowhere to keep our treasured books." She began to stroll about the room, pausing to check titles. "This is nicely organized. I see the Latin titles here, and in that last alcove, poetry."

"If you are anything like my sisters, you must love to read poetry."

She shrugged. "I fear my reading tastes are not very feminine. Because my Papa had no son, he educated me as if I were a boy."

"Don't tell me you read Latin?"

She nodded ruefully. "And German, and French."

"Your father must have been quite a scholar."

"Actually he was, though he was not fluent in French. He always regretted he had to read Rousseau in translation. He insisted I learn the language, and he spent a guinea a quarter for me to receive instruction."

Which must have been somewhat of a hardship for a poor country cleric. He watched with pleasure as she flitted from one section to another, examining titles. "So if you are not enamored of poetry, what do you read?"

"If I tell you, you will think me a most unfeminine creature."

"Try me."

"I like philosophers. Marcus Aurelius's *Meditations*, Jeremy Bentham, Rousseau, Aristotle, Burke."

He folded his hands over his chest. "Don't tell me I've married a bloody bluestocking!"

"Well, I do like Shakespeare. Will that make me seem more normal?"

His hungry gaze lingered over her: over her satin face, over the sweet swell of her breasts, along her slender fingers and down her lean trunk. She was a feast to behold. "Nothing about you, my lady, is normal."

Her cheeks turned pink. "You must tell me what you enjoy reading."

"I have to say I was astonished when the first book you mentioned was Aurelius's *Meditations* for it's a book I've read probably thirty times." His heated gaze met and held hers.

She finally looked away and strolled to the

fireplace. "You have fires in every room? It's such an expense!"

He laughed. "Not in every room. We have one hundred and twenty-three chambers at Farley—many of them no longer in use. But we do like a fire in each room that is likely to be used."

Her mouth gaped open. "One hundred and twenty-three rooms? Do you ever get lost?"

He shook his head. "It's a linear layout, most simple to navigate."

Next, they poked their heads into the morning room and old hall before he took her down a long corridor that terminated at a small, but heavily ornamented chapel.

"Oh, it's beautiful!" she exclaimed as she moved down its nave and came to kneel before the baroque crucifix that was flanked by two stained glass windows, one depicting the Nativity and the other the Ascension.

Seeing her kneeling before the altar, so solemn, so angelic, flooded him with memories of the day they had met. They had both been so forlorn that day, and he liked to think their union the following day lifted away that veil of gloom. Now here they both were, two completely different beings than they were then but so very much happier. He felt overcome by the need to kneel and pray his thanks for bringing him to St. Clement's that morning, for bringing his precious daughter into their world. He came and knelt beside her and silently prayed.

When they left the chapel several minutes later, he took her hand.

"Where has your mother moved?" She could not shake the feeling she—a woman who most certainly did not belong here—had dislodged his mother from her home.

"My father had a dowager's wing added to the rear of Farley for his mother. The bedchamber is on the first floor, so the elimination of stair climbing is desirable for one getting on in years."

"Your mother, I think, is astonishingly young."

"Yes. Thankfully it will be many years before she has to avoid climbing stairs." He squeezed her hand.

This was the first time in her one and twenty years a man had ever held her hand, and she could not understand the odd connection there was between her hand and heart, but she could not deny that the minute his hand clasped hers, her heart went to fluttering like a bat flapping its wings.

"Don't worry about displacing Mother. She's most comfortable, and she will still be close enough to share family life with us."

"You are a most stubborn creature. I have told you repeatedly we are not a family. I'm not fit to be a viscountess. You must find a way to dissolve this . . . this make-believe marriage so you can marry a proper viscountess."

He shook his head, the corners of his mouth lifting with a smile. "Shame on you. A rector's daughter who does not respect the sacred sacrament of matrimony."

"I appreciate your gallantry, my lord, but I am inflexible on my resolve to return to my previous modest life."

"I thought you were most at home in both the library and the chapel."

"How could anyone not warm to those very special places?"

"There is Fanny to consider. You do not want to give her up, and I believe here at Farley Manor as my ward, she can be raised as I think you would wish for her to."

"You're most odious."

"You would wish for me to ignore my child's existence?"

She did not know what she wanted. For Fanny, yes, she knew he was right. Fanny belonged at Farley Manor. She deserved to be raised with the privilege his lordship could offer. And the maddening man knew she would never leave her child. But why would he be willing to forgo any chance of true love to saddle himself with a simple parson's daughter?

They continued down another long corridor, this one made of oak that had turned dark with age and worn smooth by Tate footsteps over the centuries. "Did you sleep well?" he asked.

"Indeed, I did. I have never experienced a more cozy feeling. I shall miss sleeping with Fanny when she returns to the nursery."

"You do realize, my lady, that Farley is reaching out and wrapping you in its comforting embrace?"

Dear heavens, he spoke the truth! Even though her mind kept telling her she didn't belong, her heart told her quite the opposite.

"I've spoken to Susan about procuring a nurse for Fanny and a maid for you."

She stopped in mid stride. "Whatever would I need a maid for?"

"You shall have to ask my sister about that. I believe they assist one with dressing and look after their clothing. Things of that sort."

"My lord, I possess but two dresses!"

"That does reflect most poorly upon your husband. Have I not been generous enough to you?"

"I told you before, I go nowhere, therefore I don't need an extensive wardrobe."

"But all that has changed with the change of your husband's status."

She liked it better when her husband was just Harry, a captain in the Guards. She had to confess she had fanaticized about him returning and falling in love with her and making a real home for her and Fanny.

But this wasn't the Harry she'd half fallen in love with. This was an aristocrat from a world in which she could never belong.

Even if she had fallen completely in love with her purple bedchamber. And the warm library. And the baroque chapel.

"Oh, there you are!" Susan said, scurrying toward them, then hooking her arm through Elizabeth's. "You will be happy to learn all of my commissions have been successfully completed."

Her brother raised a brow. "You've already procured a nurse and a lady's maid?"

"Indeed I have." She peered up at her brother. "Nothing would do when Na Na heard there was to be a child at Farley again that she must come out of retirement and care for it."

"Na Na was nurse to all of us," he explained to Elizabeth, "and she's continued living here."

"And she's not been happy to have been put to pasture," Susan added. "She adores children, and she wants nothing more than to be useful." She turned to Elizabeth. "You could never have a more loving woman to care for your child than Na Na."

"I couldn't be more pleased," he said. "And

what of the lady's maid?"

"I wanted to speak with Lady Broxbourne first."

Elizabeth most certainly did not like to be addressed as such. It did so sound like his mother's name.

"Would you object to training one?'

Elizabeth broke out into laughter. "It would be like the blind leading the blind."

"My wife does not perceive that she needs a maid."

"Oh, but you will, my dear, once we've finished with your new wardrobe." Susan's gaze shifted from Elizabeth to Harry. "If you're finished with her, the girls and I are going to attack any wardrobe deficiencies she may have."

"I do need to meet with Hinckley now," he said, making eye contact with Elizabeth, "but I was hoping this afternoon to show you some of the grounds."

"But everything's covered with snow," Susan protested.

"There's still much to see."

Elizabeth glared at him. "Whatever you say, my lord."

He started to stroll away. "And, Susan, make sure my wife gets at least a dozen new dresses."

Susan began to lead Elizabeth away. "How very exciting."

Elizabeth's face was scorched by the realization she was an embarrassment to Harry and his family because of her dowdy clothing.

Chapter 4

The library door eased open. He was disappointed it was only Susan. He'd wished to be alone in the warmth of this comforting chamber with his wife.

"Here you are!" Susan came and sat on a sofa near him.

"You've been fitting my wife for new gowns, no doubt?" It did not matter to him what Elizabeth wore, she was always lovely. Extraordinarily so.

"It has been so much fun. Can you believe the dear woman appears to be completely unaware of how exquisitely, unbelievably beautiful she is?"

"She does seem to lack artifice of any kind."

"We were able to take a couple of Diane's dresses and hem them to fit your petite wife until the new ones can be made. She will quite put the rest of us to shame at the dinner table tonight. "

He should argue, but to do so would be to lie. "Let's just say our table will be blessed with the loveliest ladies in all of Derbyshire tonight."

"Aren't you diplomatic!" His sister's eyes narrowed. "I must know about the child. As much of a rake as you have been, dear brother, seducing clergymen's daughters was not one of your vices. I thought you only went for opera dancers."

His sister was too damned perceptive. He'd never been able to hide anything from her. "The opera dancer died in childbed with Fanny." The very mention of Annie's death still scraped a deep wound inside him.

"Oh, Harry, I'm so sorry."

"I was fortunate to find a clergyman's daughter to look after my daughter."

"A clergyman's daughter who just happens to be excruciatingly lovely."

He nodded. "She's out of charity with me now, though."

"Why?"

"Because I wasn't honest with her. She did not know my father was a viscount."

"And that upsets her? How many women have thrown themselves at your feet in the hopes of being your viscountess someday?"

"I think she could have been happy as the wife of a captain in the Guards, but she says she is not fit to be the wife of a viscount."

"That's positively ridiculous. A sweet-natured thing like she would bring credit to our family."

He knew he could always count on Susan. "Would that Mama would be less rigid with her."

"She will. It just takes time. She was not happy that your wife gave birth to a child out of wedlock—or so she thought. May I tell her the truth?"

"I know I should be the one to tell her, but I just can't bring up the topic of opera dancers with my own mother."

"Leave it to me." She gave him a rather queer look. "Tell me, Harry, are you in love with Elizabeth?"

He had not tried to put to words this tangle of feelings the fair Elizabeth evoked in him. "If wanting to spend every minute with her and being unable to purge her from my mind when we're apart, then, yes, I suppose I am."

Despite what she thought, his wife made a wonderful viscountess. He could not remove his gaze from her throughout dinner. Not only did she look stunning in a saffron colored gown of a very sheer fabric, but her solicitousness of the others at the table could not have been more genuine.

"Do you not find your wife's hair lovely, Broxbourne?" Susan asked.

"Is that why I haven't been able to take my eyes off her?" He smiled mischievously at Elizabeth.

"Her new lady's maid dressed it for her."

His mother directed her attention to Susan. "I wasn't aware of this."

"I took the liberty of elevating one of the chambermaids that I had noticed had a flair for dressing her own hair," Susan explained.

"You would not believe how thrilled she was to become a lady's maid," Sarah added.

"Which chambermaid?" the dowager asked.

"Newman."

"Whom I shall now address as Sally," Elizabeth said. "She's ever so competent, even though I am certainly no judge."

"You were lovely before," the dowager said, "and you're even lovelier now."

He could have lifted his mother into his arms and swung her around the chamber.

"I'm sorry we stole your wife for the whole afternoon," Susan said to Harry, "but we were all having such fun with the new dress patterns and taking fittings and selecting fabric. I hope you weren't too disappointed. I know you wanted to show your wife the grounds this afternoon."

"As it happens, my business with Hinckley

took much longer than I expected." He looked at Elizabeth. "Will you work me into your schedule in the morning?"

"It will be my pleasure."

"In the afternoon I was hoping we could take the children to gather fresh berries to decorate the house for Christmas," his mother said.

"They will love that," Susan said.

"I know Fanny will. She was scarcely more than a babe last Christmas," Elizabeth said. There was a tenderness in her voice and a sparkle in her eyes when she talked about Fanny.

"Have you seen the nursery?" Susan asked Elizabeth.

"Only for a few seconds this morning when we were looking for your boys. It was quite empty."

"Let's go there after dinner," he suggested. "You'll want to meet Na Na."

"Oh, I already met her. A lovely old woman, she is. Fanny was immediately taken with her. I shall become most jealous."

"So," Robert said to his oldest friend, "your wife tells us you met at church. 'Pon my word, I almost fell over when I heard that."

Just like his wife, Robert was too damned nosey. And it was too bloody hard to hide anything from either of them. Harry's gaze flicked down the length of the table to where his viscountess graced their presence with her elegance. "So, what did you tell them about our meeting?"

"I told them you were most solemn—and that I believed you to be pious."

Robert's bellowing laugh was contagious.

Elizabeth and his mother exchanged imploring gazes. "They just don't understand Har-,

Broxbourne's finer qualities."

His mother offered Elizabeth her tight smile. "Indeed they don't, my dear."

From the day she'd gotten Fanny, they had never been separated. She had been so happy this morning for Fanny to have found a little playmate, but she was slightly wounded that Fanny wasn't a bit more clingy.

It was going to be torture for her to leave her child in the nursery each night. It was so very far from her own chambers. She knew Na Na would be there with her and would take good care of her, but Elizabeth was beginning to feel as if she were not needed anymore. Just what was she bringing to this marriage now?

She had feared that Fanny would be upset at their separation and was bitter sweetly surprised when she was not. Of course, as long as her cousins were staying at Farley, the three of them would all sleep in the big nursery, along with Na Na.

What child wouldn't love the nursery? The huge chamber was probably as large as Papa's church, only it was informally divided into various areas. Her heart tugged when she saw a baby cradle in a corner. Had Harry used that when he was a wee one? Another area was like a small school room with little tables and chairs and a bookcase brimming with dog-eared volumes. One corner held a couple of large laundry-sized baskets brimming with toys, and another featured rows of plump, undersized feather beds.

While Elizabeth set all the children around her while she read them a bedtime story, Susan nearly tore up the room searching for Helene. "Na

Na," Susan asked, "do you not know where Helene is?"

The plump, gray-haired woman shook her head. "I 'aven't seen that doll since Diane decided she liked boys better than dolls."

"I did so want for Fanny to have her," Susan said.

Elizabeth was touched over how sweet Susan had been to her—and to Fanny. All of her husband's sisters had been exceedingly kind. It made her feel even worse, knowing she was a fraud.

To her delight, when she finished reading to the children, his lordship sat on the edge of Fanny's bed and proceeded to tell the children a story he knew by heart. It was the story of David and Goliath, and he told it with great inflection. The children were spellbound.

When he finished, they all implored him to tell them another. "Tomorrow night," he promised. He tucked the covers around Fanny and bent to kiss the top of her head. "Sleep tight, Little Love."

While he was tucking Fanny in, Susan kissed each of her sons.

Before they left the chamber, Elizabeth pressed a kiss to Fanny's cheek.

To her astonishment, Fanny did not even take notice of her leaving. One half of Elizabeth was thrilled that Fanny was enjoying her cousins and all the new experiences so thoroughly, but the other half of her wished she was back in their little cottage on the outskirts of London, where it had just been the two of them—and her dreams of one day sharing that cottage with her dashing captain when he returned from the Peninsula.

Now she felt as unneeded as a third leg.

* * *

After dinner he had gallantly offered to partner with his wife at whist against Susan and Robert, but it turned out to be no sacrifice at all. His wife was an excellent whist player. As much as he enjoyed the game, though, he kept wishing the game over, wishing he could be alone with her before the fire in her bedchamber.

When Susan began yawning uncontrollably, he was happy to terminate play. "It's been a long day," he said, reaching to pat his sister on the back. "Early to bed is a good idea."

He did not miss Robert's sly glance from him to Elizabeth and the little smirk on his old friend's mouth.

As they climbed the stairs in the cool stairwell, he proffered his arm to Elizabeth and began to stroke the length of her glove. "Cold?"

"It does get terribly cold here."

"I should have an inglenook installed," he said, leaning toward her, then speaking mischievously. "But then I wouldn't have an excuse to take you arm in such an intimate gesture."

She snatched her arm away as if stung by a bee. "You odious man!" The humorous flash in her eyes belied her words.

When they reached the door to her chamber, he said, "May I come in? There are a few matters I wish to discuss with you."

"Of course." She strolled into the chamber. "Won't you sit on the settee, my lord?"

"Now see here, Elizabeth! I'm your husband. Must you be so beastly formal?" He waved her to sit first. A gentleman did not sit while a lady stood.

"I am sorry if I don't know what is expected of

me." She sat down at the far end of the silken settee. "I've told you countless times I'm not fit to be your wife."

"You're the only one possessed of that opinion."

"You're much too kind, but I've always been aware of your excessive nobility."

"Pray, do not imbue me with qualities I do not possess." A truly noble man would not have dalliances with opera dancers he had no intentions of marrying. For that, he would atone for the rest of his days.

"What are these matters you wished to discuss?"

"I wanted to let you know that Susan knows everything about Fanny's parentage, and when Susan knows something, everyone at Farley is soon informed.

Her pretty little face was pensive, her long lashes lowered as she contemplated his words.

"Does that displease you?"

There was incredible sadness on her face when she looked up at him. "I have most terribly mixed emotions. I am happy that your family knows I did not give birth out of wedlock, but I'm unbelievably sad to relinquish that maternal claim on the child I think of as my own."

His hand covered hers, and he squeezed. "A mother is measured in many ways, and by any manner that counts, you are Fanny's mother. That is one of the things I wished to discuss with you tonight."

"What?"

"What we will tell Fanny—when she's much older, of course."

An incredible sadness penetrated those limpid blue eyes of hers.

"I see no reason why she ever need know the truth of her origins—as far as the opera dancer goes. Beastly, I know. But you are the only mother she's ever known, and I assure you, you would be the mother she would have selected."

She flicked away a tear that had begun to trail down her cheek. "That's very kind of you."

He lifted her hand to his lips for a tender kiss. "If it's for kindness, it's only for kindness to my daughter."

"Of course."

"Does my recommendation meet with your approval?"

"Indeed, it does, but what will you tell her about her . . . male parent?"

"You are probably not as familiar with the practice of having natural children, coming from your ecclesiastic background, but in our circle the natural father is understood but never referred to in any other way than as guardian to ward."

"Anyone who looks at her will be able to ascertain who her father is."

A smile hitched across his face as he shrugged.

"Is there anything more you wish to discuss?" she asked.

"I suppose not," he said, rising. He began to walk to his connecting chamber door, then stopped, turned back, and strolled to the settee where she still sat. He lowered his head to hers and settled his lips over hers for a lingering kiss. "Good night, dear wife." Pulling away from her sweet, yielding lips was one of the hardest things he'd ever done.

When he reached the doorway he turned back and gave her a wicked smile. "If your bed needs warming, I'll be happy to oblige."

"Out, you odious man!"

Trembles overlapping more trembles seized her entire body. Except for the chaste kiss on the morning of her wedding, she had never been kissed before. She was completely unprepared for the magnitude of her reaction to it. How could so simple a physical gesture so profoundly affect both mind and body?

Not only was she overwhelmed by the numbing emotions the kiss evoked, she was also stunned over her initial reaction to it. She had enjoyed it! She had fully participated in it! And she'd even wanted to prolong it! Oh, dear, would his lordship think her a doxy?

Long after Sally helped her into her night shift and closed the heavy velvet draperies around her bed, Elizabeth lay there in the utter darkness thinking about the man who was her husband. She was so completely confused. For so long now she had dreamed of her dashing captain—the man she had prayed so fervently for these past two years—coming home and settling with her and Fanny in their little cottage. Then she'd learned he was no simple army captain, but a viscount with an ancestral home the size of the entire village of Upper Frampington. Now the gap between them was too large to bridge. She would never belong in his world.

She began to cry. The pity of it all was, now that he had kissed her, she knew she would never want any other man.

For hours she lay there in turmoil. Then she realized what she must do. She must take a page from his own book of nobility. She must sacrifice her own happiness for the good of those she loved.

For she had come to accept that she was, indeed, in love with Harold Tate, Viscount Broxbourne.

In order for him to find true happiness with a woman of his own kind, Elizabeth must leave.

Chapter 5

Lord Broxbourne—she tried not to think of him as Harry now that he held so exalted a title—collected her in a horse-drawn sleigh built for just two as soon as she finished her morning toast. The skies were gray, the weather frigid. Her first thought upon stepping onto Farley's portico and seeing the clouds of cold air dance around her nose was perhaps she should not allow Fanny to gather greenery later that afternoon. She did not want her to take a cold.

Elizabeth wore a thick, hooded cape of faded claret colored wool, its hood trimmed with white rabbit fur that matched her muff. Would his family find her cloak embarrassing? No doubt his mother and sisters possessed muffs of ermine.

When his lordship took her hand to help her into the sleigh and when his other hand settled at her waist, that beastly fluttering in the vicinity of her heart commenced again. The sooner she got away from this man and his seductive touch, the better.

For every day spent in his company made her love him just a little bit more.

And, she had discovered, love was a most painful emotion.

The sleigh was pulled by a single white horse which was in no great hurry. His lordship flicked the ribbons with hands sheathed in beautifully made fine leather gloves. His boots, too, were made of soft brown leather. She found it ironic that his woolen muffler matched her cape. Except his claret was not faded.

It suddenly struck her that even though they had supposedly been married for more than two years, she had never before sat so close to him, never before been so aware of his manliness. His greatcoat flapped open in the front to reveal two muscled thighs that were twice the size of hers.

Against all her resolve and in complete contrast to her heretofore exceedingly chaste existence, Elizabeth thought of his last words to her the night before. "*If your bed needs warming, I will be happy to oblige.*" She found herself wondering what it would be like to lie with him, to feel his lips on hers, to feel his hands on her bare flesh.

The very thought fissured her heart.

"Are you cold?" he asked a short time later.

"Of course, I'm cold. It is snowing."

He chuckled. "For someone who looks like an angel, you can be blisteringly honest."

"Is it wrong to prize honesty?"

"It must not be because I know the parson's daughter would not do anything that was not right."

Despite the nobility of his character, he must really be dwelling on her humble origins. Why else would he keep referring to her father's vocation? "It was my father who was the holy man."

"Then you're telling me you're not holy? Come, come, Elizabeth, I don't believe you."

Hearing her Christian name upon his lips sounded so intimate. It stirred something deep inside her. "All right. I suppose I am respectably religious, and I assure you, I've brought up Fanny to go to church every Sunday and to say her prayers every night."

"I could not have found a better mother for Fanny than you have been."

She prayed he would not see her eyes moisten. "Thank you, my lord. It has always been my object to be as good of a mother as was possible."

"Oh, I forgot to tell you about Fanny's Christmas present."

She felt wretched she had left London in such a hurry, she had not gotten her daughter a toy to celebrate the birth of their Savior. "Pray, my lord, what is it?"

"I've commissioned my steward's wife to make Fanny a muff from rabbit hair. She said she can have it finished by this afternoon."

"You make me feel wretched. I have nothing to give her." But she was pleased that he would not be embarrassed over using a common fur like rabbit. She found a small measure of satisfaction that she was not quite as dowdy as she'd thought.

"Then we shall say the muff comes from you," he suggested.

"We will say no such thing," she protested. "I despise lying. And deceit. Besides, I think it an excellent idea for you to do everything you can to ingratiate yourself with your daughter."

"Like telling her bedtime stories?"

She turned to him, her smile wide and her eyes flashing with mirth. "All the children enjoyed your story ever so much last night. Even though I've read the story hundreds of times, I even enjoyed it. You're a remarkable storyteller."

"I like being with children." He flicked a smiling glance to her. "I gave those epaulets to the lads this morning."

"I would have loved to have seen their faces."

"They're great lads. Remarkable how much Robbie looks like me."

"Indeed. He and Fanny could easily pass as brother and sister."

"Speaking of sisters, what do you think of now having three?"

It made her heart ache. Her entire life she had lamented that she had no sisters, and now she had three wonderful sisters, but she must leave them. How it would hurt! Susan had won her admiration with her generous heart, and Sarah with her love of many of the same books Elizabeth poured over, and pretty Diana with her exhilarating exuberance was a delight to be around. "I wish I could be with each of them always."

"I will miss Susan when she returns to Woodhead, and Mother and I both will miss Sarah and Diana when they marry and leave."

She would wager his mother would not enjoy having to live at Farley with no other female than she.

"I wish you could see Farley in the spring when everything's green and the rhododendron are in bloom."

Her gaze fanned across the barren trees and hills and dales blanketed with crisp white snow. "Winter has its own charm—provided one is properly bundled and doesn't actually have to trod through the snow."

He turned north and pulled to a stop. "I wanted you to see Farley from this view."

She was overwhelmed by the sight of the stately home rising from a smooth bed of white, smoke curling from its many chimneys. Despite its vast size, it presented an incredibly comforting presence. "Oh, my lord." Without realizing what she was doing, she began to stroke his forearm. "It's so lovely."

His arm enclosed her, and once again his head lowered to hers for a thorough kiss. And, once again, she could no more stop the kiss than she could stop loving Fanny. She had fallen slave to her feelings.

When she finally summoned enough presence of mind to realize what a complete goose she was, she pulled away from him and made a display of arranging loose strands of her flaxen locks.

He did not relinquish his hold on her. His face close to hers, he whispered huskily. "Your new home my lady. I hope you will one day love it as much as I do."

She had never thought she would like so large a house, but she found so much of Farley comforting. How she would hate to leave it now! How she would hate to return to her cottage alone.

But she knew what she had to do. Because she loved him. She had to allow him free choice of a wife. Dear, noble soul that he was.

"It's a wonderful home," she said, afraid each second that she would burst into tears. "It's very much a family home." *Too bad I'm not part of that family.*

Even if Fanny was.

He took up the ribbons again and headed to the folly, a decidedly Palladian structure on a slight mound that he explained overlooked the lake.

"There's a lake here?" she asked.

He nodded. "It's frozen over. When we were little we often skated on it—until Susan fell through the ice and nearly froze to death before we could get her out."

"That must have been terrifying."

"Especially for Sue. Papa never let us skate after that."

"It sounds as if he was exercising his fatherly authority well."

"Spoken like a true mother." He took the reins again. "Allow me to show you the mews. They're our pride and joy. Do you know, I've never asked if you ride."

"What is your guess?"

"My guess is that you don't."

"You are correct, my lord. Keeping a horse in an expense a clergyman cannot afford." She was not in the least ashamed of her background; she merely wanted him to be able to choose a woman from his own world.

"If you are not afraid of the beasts, it would be my pleasure to teach you to ride."

He was so kindly. "I expect you're a Corinthian."

"You will have to judge for yourself one day—when you have enough knowledge to make that distinction."

As their sleigh continued to cut its path through the crisp, fresh snow, she looked ahead at a two-story stone edifice. "Do not tell me that building is the mews! Why, it's larger than both my Papa's house and church put together."

"That is the mews we're so proud of." The horse leading their sleigh just trotted right through the open door. Elizabeth was astonished that all of this could possibly belong to one family. The first chamber they passed housed a luxurious carriage, a phaeton, and a larger sleigh. Then came the actual stables where horses of every color were stalled. There must be at least thirty. "You must show me which horse is yours, my lord."

He came to a stop, leapt down, then assisted her. Taking her hand, he led her to a stall midway down. "Isn't she a beaut?"

Elizabeth did not know the first thing about horses. All she could tell was that his horse was very large, very black, and had the most beautiful white ankles and hooves. Did horses even have ankles? "Oh, she really is! It looks as if she's wearing white boots."

"I've been gone so long, it's a wonder she hasn't been put to pasture." He patted the beast lovingly.

The horse responded to his touch with a whinnying noise.

"She remembers you!"

"Should you like me to saddle 'er, milord?" the groom asked.

Harry spun around to face the young man who was probably not yet twenty. "Jeremy? My God, boy, you've grown a foot!" He offered his hand to the groom, and they shook hands like a pair of men on equal footing.

"It's mighty good to 'ave ye back, milord."

Her husband turned to her. "Lady Broxbourne, may I present Jeremy? He's spent his entire life at Farley, and nobody knows horses better."

The groom bowed, and they exchanged greetings.

"Actually," Harry said, "neither of us will ride today, Jeremy. I just wanted to show my bride the stables."

His lordship set his hand to her waist and led her back to the sleigh. "This afternoon, we'll need the big sleigh brought around to the house. I promised the children a bruising sleigh ride."

"Don't forget to bring the rugs," Jeremy cautioned as they were led from the stable.

Neither she nor her husband spoke on the way back to Farley. She was so utterly content, she was not aware of the cold anymore. Nothing had ever affected her as profoundly as riding beside this man she so admired. So loved. How fortunate would be the woman he would select to share his life with.

Elizabeth was to discover that in the Tate family the gathering of greenery was limited to women and children. Susan had informed her that their husbands were in the billiard parlor.

Elizabeth felt ever so shabby in her faded red cloak next the real Lady Broxbourne whose cloak was trimmed in ermine, just as Elizabeth had surmised. Susan's was almost identical to her mother's, and the two youngest sisters wore velvet capes that were lined with a soft white fur she had never before seen. Each of them looked exquisite. And Elizabeth felt as attractive as a chimneysweep.

Jeremy had brought around both the large sleigh and the small one. "Come with me," Susan said to Elizabeth. "I'll drive the big one, and you can sit beside me. Mama will sit in the back with the children on her lap."

Sarah and Diana hopped onto the small sleigh, and they all took off for the holly bower just south of the folly. As Susan drove the pair of matched grays, Elizabeth faced backward to watch Fanny. Lady Broxbourne had Fanny on her right knee and Tommy on her left. Their smiling faces bracing against the wind, each of them wore woolen mittens, thick wool coats, and bright red mufflers. Their grandmother had spread the rug over their laps and that of Robbie, who sat beside her.

When they reached the holly bower, the dowager demonstrated to the children how to snap off useful pieces of Christmas greenery.

Fanny attempted to listen to her grandmother, but she had no idea of what they were trying to accomplish. She was most interested in the little red balls. She snapped one off and went to put it in her mouth.

"Oh, no, no," Lady Broxbourne said, removing it from her mouth and throwing it away.

"No, no," Fanny said, snapping off another and throwing it the ground.

Elizabeth smiled to herself as Harry's mother carefully explained to Fanny what they were doing. Susan and Tommy went ahead a bit and began to collect boughs.

"Why do you not look for some pine cones, Robbie?" his grandmother suggested.

He scurried off.

Elizabeth once again felt as useless as a third leg, but she was overjoyed that Lady Broxbourne was accepting Fanny so thoroughly.

It was obvious that Fanny belonged at Farley Manor, obvious that she adored her cousins, and they seemed taken with her, too. Elizabeth could not have hoped for Fanny to have received a more hearty welcome.

She set about gathering some larger pieces of holly to augment the meager snatches Tommy and Fanny were gathering.

She heard Robbie exclaim as he began to chase

as black kitten that scurried off away from him toward the folly.

She knew there was no way a five-year-old lad could catch the speedier cat, but she wished he could for she knew Fanny would love to hold the kitten.

A minute later she thought she heard a child's cry. Her heartbeat thumped. She dropped her greenery and straightened up instantly from bending over a bush, her gaze arrowing straight to Fanny. Fanny was fine. Her little face was screwed up with great seriousness as she concentrated on her task of severing a limb of holly.

Elizabeth gathered the greenery she had dropped and began to return to her task when she heard a second cry. This one of desperation.

This time she knew something was wrong with Robbie, and she started for the folly.

From some distance behind her, Elizabeth heard Susan's strangled cry. "Robbie! Robbie!"

"This way!" Elizabeth said, racing off toward the direction of the child's cries. As soon as she broke free of the bower, she realized what must have happened.

Robbie had broken through the ice and fallen into the icy lake.

"Go for a rope!" Elizabeth instructed as she sped forward.

Within the sea of stark white snow, all she could see was a tiny hand waving.

From fifty yards behind her, she heard Susan's anguish. "Oh, my God, he's fallen in the lake!"

Elizabeth knew if the thin ice could not support a five-year-old child, it would not support them. She threw off her heavy woolen cloak. She was the best hope of saving the child since she was easily the smallest adult. And her father had made sure she knew how to swim. If she could just get to him in time, she could tread water, holding him, until someone could toss them a rope and pull them away.

She ran as fast as her legs could propel her, and when she got to within twenty feet of the child—now she could see the top of his dark head as it plunged beneath the surface of the frigid water—she lay on the ice and began to slither toward the break in the ice in order to better distribute her weight.

The cold shocked her system. Pain pulsed from the outside in. Her flesh felt as if it were burning. She began to shiver uncontrollably.

She kept watching the hole in the ice, the place where she'd last seen his tiny hand as it plunged beneath the water's surface.

"Don't Susan! You're too heavy!" warned Lady Broxbourne. "Let Elizabeth get him. You go for a rope."

"No, I will!" Sarah called. "Be careful Elizabeth."

By now Elizabeth was numb to her own discomfort. Her only thoughts were of getting the boy. He had been underwater for several seconds. She decided speed was more important now than finesse. She put her weight to her knees and went to stand up when the ice cracked, then broke into shards, plunging her beneath the surface.

She flailed about in the water, feeling for Robbie. But she got nothing except for fists of piercingly cold water. She knew she would have to go head first next time. This time she would go against her natural instinct—which was to close her eyes against water—and open them beneath the icy surface of the lake, praying she would be able to see Robbie before it was too late.

Her first plunge, all she saw was blackness. The sheet of ice over the lake kept light from penetrating. Her heartbeat galloped at the same time her stomach sickened. She was not going to find him.

She found the cutaway hole and came up to draw deep waves of air into her exploding lungs before she plunged back underwater again. This time she rocketed herself lower, her arms flailing wildly, praying her hands would come in contact with the precious little boy before it was too late.

Please, God. Please.

That very second, she felt him. She still could not see him. It was too dark. She enclosed one arm around him and kicked against the heavy water, propelling both of them toward the area of light.

She barely had enough air left in her lungs to make it. Breaking the water's surface, she gulped for air at the same time as she elevated Robbie's lifeless head above hers. He still did not move. "Dear God, no!" she cried.

And that very second, he started coughing.

No sound had ever been more welcome. Now, she could call for that bloody rope! "Help!"

If help did not come soon, both of them would freeze to death. They were half way there already. Her body shivered so savagely, her teeth cut her lips.

Despite her size, her strong legs allowed her to continue treading water with little effort, but her arms were extremely tired from holding Robbie above her shoulders. She couldn't last much longer.

Then she heard Harry's voice.

CHAPTER 6

He refused to leave her side even though he knew she was not in grave condition. His mother had seen to it that she dressed warmly and stayed beneath the blankets to bring up her body temperature. She'd been in that cold water for so damn long.

For a brief few minutes that afternoon, he'd thought he lost her. He hoped to God he never again had to endure anything as painful as that. During those moments, he lamented that he'd never told her how much she had come to mean to him, never told her he had fallen in love with her. He meant to tell her now.

"I wish your family would quit treating me as if I'm a heroine," she told him as he sat on the edge of her bed, holding her hand.

"First, love, it is not *my* family. It's our family. For better or worse, you're part of us."

There was a knock on her chamber door. "It's Susan. May I come in?"

"Of course," he said.

Sniffling, his eldest sister entered the chamber. His heart went out to her. She'd become hysterical when her firstborn had fallen into the frigid lake. Not only was she paralyzed with fear, but she was likely traumatized by reliving the same horrifying accident from her own youth.

She came straight to the bed. "Oh, Elizabeth, my dearest sister, I had to come and tell you how very glad I am to have you in our family. If it hadn't been for you, I'd have lost my precious Robbie—and no telling how many of us would have perished trying to save him."

Elizabeth shook her head and went to protest, but her husband cut her off.

"She's right, my dear," he said, kissing her hand. "You were the only person in the group who knew how to swim."

"She had such wonderful presence of mind," Susan said.

"How is it," he asked his wife, "you *do* know how to swim? It doesn't seem to be a skill many ladies seem to possess."

"My papa. He must have wanted a son most badly for he was constantly treating me as one does a son." Elizabeth laughed to herself. "I remember him telling me that my ability to swim might save someone's life one day. How is poor little Robbie?"

"He's beneath the blankets, and his teeth are still chattering, but he's going to be just fine. Robert and I are so profoundly grateful to you."

Elizabeth gathered her blue shawl closer around her as a shiver sent her shaking. "I'm ever so grateful that my husband got there in time—and with a rope—to get us out of there."

Susan's gaze flicked to his. "I did not know my dear husband was possessed of such deep emotions. Did you, Broxbourne?"

Though he had known Robert since he was eight years of age, today was the first time he'd ever seen him cry. Tears welled in his own eyes when he thought of losing his own loved one. Elizabeth. "I doubt there was a dry eye there today."

Susan reached out and patted him. "The children—minus Robbie—are going to decorate the drawing room with fresh greenery this evening. We're going to allow Robbie to lie on the sofa near the fire and watch. I would like to request the footmen to place two sofas near the fire, the other for you, my lady."

"Will you feel up to it, love?" he asked Elizabeth, his voice tender.

"I wouldn't miss it."

Harry's eyes had moistened! How very touching that he loved his nephew so. Since the day she had met him, she had understood that this rugged, privileged man was possessed of a tender heart. And a nobility of spirit. And a generous soul.

She was touched at his concern for her, too. Just when she was feeling as if she were as worthless as ashes in the hearth, he had the ability to make her feel. . . valued? How could that be?

"I'm glad we're finally alone," he said after Susan departed. His husky voice held a note that had not been there before. Not ever.

Truth to tell, she was glad to be alone with him. She would like to imagine this a real marriage, if only for a few moments. What would it be like to allow herself to love him? The very notion sent her heartbeat roaring, her stomach plummeting, and her lower body stirring in a way she had never experienced. She gazed into his black eyes. "Me, too."

He squeezed her hand. "This afternoon, for a few minutes, I thought I'd lost you."

Had she heard him correctly? Her eyes

widened. She was afraid to breathe, afraid she might miss his next words because of the roaring of her heart.

"And all I could think of," he continued, his voice low and uneven, "was I never told you how much I . . ." He swallowed. "I love you."

Surely she was dreaming! Or had the depth of her own feelings made her hear what she wanted to hear, not what he really said? She could not remove her eyes—which were now filling with tears—from his. Had he really just said he was in love with her? "You love me?" her voice squeaked like a child's. What a pathetic viscountess she made!

"I think I knew it that morning I left you at St. Clement's, right after we exchanged vows. Walking away from you that day was one of the hardest things I've ever done. Time after time, I picked up my pen to write you, but I thought it would be too cruel to both of us, given my belief that---"

"---that you were going to die." Tears streamed down her face as she squeezed both his hands.

"Now that you've come into my life again," he murmured, "I never want us to separate. I've wanted to be with you every waking minute."

She flung herself into his arms, weeping with joy. "Oh, Harry, my dearest love, I do love you!"

Now that she was enclosed within her husband's arms, she was finally warm.

His mother was enjoying decorating the drawing room with greenery even more than her two little grandchildren she was supposedly assisting. Why was it, he wondered, her icy countenance melted when she was with the children? He could not have been more pleased at the way she had taken to his precious little Fanny.

What a wonderful home Farley Manor was going to be for her, surrounded by so many who loved her. And soon, he hoped, she would have brothers and sisters. His breath hitched at the memory of how thoroughly he and his wife had loved that afternoon.

"Comfortable, my love?" he asked Elizabeth, who reclined on a sofa, her husband at her side, near the blazing fire.

The glow of the smile on her flawless face could brighten the darkest room. "Never more so."

"Mama!" Fanny ran up to them, excitedly. "Milady says I'm to get a present!" Milady was the name the grandchildren had adopted for his mother.

"That's wonderful," Elizabeth said.

Though he was certainly not impartial, he thought Fanny the loveliest little girl he had ever seen. Her short, dark curls framed a delicate ivory face that was tinged with pink cheeks. Though her dark eyes were his eyes, he did not possess the uncommonly long lashes this beautiful creature did. In the firelight, her hair glistened with a mahogany tint. From her lovely red velvet dress trimmed in white lace, it was obvious Elizabeth spared no expense when dressing Fanny even though she had cut corners with her own wardrobe. He went to set his daughter on his lap.

She shook her head. "Not now, milord, I must help milady." She was so utterly serious, he had to laugh as she rejoined his mother "to help."

It was all he could do not to laugh when she

offered his mother meager little twigs with a barely a holly berry on them, yet his mother praised her for her "help."

"I have some, too," Tommy said, standing beside Fanny and thrusting his offering at his grandmother.

Collins brought warm mulled wine, and Elizabeth sat up to take her cup.

A moment later, Collins brought his mother a package tied with string and a much smaller velvet box. His mother eyed Elizabeth. "I know we will exchange presents on Christ's birthday in the morning, but tonight I wish to present the newest members of our family with . . . well, you'll soon discover what!" She lifted the larger box that was tied with a string. "This is for you, Fanny."

Her little face alight, Fanny ran to her grandmother.

"Would you like me to help you open it?" his mother asked.

Her head bobbed as her tiny fingers pulled on the string. The dowager slipped it off and tore into the paper, allowing Fanny to remove the rest of it.

Fanny managed to lift off the box's top, then exclaimed, "A doll! She's beautiful!"

Even though the doll had on a brand new dress made of golden silk and her hair had obviously been either restyled or replaced, he recognized it. Susan had toted her "Helene" around for years. That porcelain-faced doll had been like a member of their family.

"Helene!" Susan exclaimed. "I looked for her because I wanted Fanny to have her."

Fanny hugged the doll.

His mother beamed at Fanny. "I have been saving her for a special little girl."

It hurt him that his mother would not be able to formally acknowledge Fanny as her granddaughter, but it was for the child's benefit.

"Where did you get Helene's beautiful new dress?" Susan asked.

His mother's blue eyes sparkled. "I made it last night, especially for Fanny."

"She's really, really mine?" Fanny asked, looking up at her grandmother.

"Yes, she is. Her name is Helene." His mother faced Elizabeth and extended the velvet box. "And this belongs to the new viscountess."

Elizabeth opened the small velvet case. He was nearly overcome with emotion when he saw that it held his mother's diamond and sapphire wedding ring.

"Every Viscountess Broxbourne has worn this ring, my dear," the dowager said to his beloved wife.

"Oh, my," was all Elizabeth could say as her eyes once again began to fill with tears.

"Allow me, my dearest," he said, taking the ring and slipping it on the same finger with the simple gold band he'd placed there two years earlier. To his astonishment, it fit her perfectly.

He should have known it would. From the minute he'd met Elizabeth, he'd had the feeling a power stronger than either of them was guiding him to her, guiding her to him and Fanny, guiding her to Farley Manor.

"The luckiest day of my life was the day we found each other at St. Clement's," he told her in a throaty voice. "You are my perfect viscountess."

"I am the luckiest lady in the kingdom."

Hi joy was complete when Fanny—and Helene—came and climbed upon his lap. This

Christmas at Farley Manor was the happiest Christmas ever.

The End

Author's Biography

A former journalist who, in her own words, has "a fascination with dead Englishwomen," Cheryl Bolen is the award-winning author of more than a dozen historical romance novels set in Regency England, including *Marriage of Inconvenience*, *My Lord Wicked*, and *A Duke Deceived*. Her books have received numerous awards, such as the 2011 International Digital Award for Best Historical Novel and the 2006 Holt Medallion for Best Historical. She was also a 2006 finalist in the Daphne du Maurier for Best Historical Mystery. Her works have been translated into eleven languages and have been Amazon.com bestsellers. Bolen has contributed to *Writers Digest* and *Romance Writers Report* as well as to the Regency era–themed newsletters *The Regency Plume, The Regency Reader*, and *The Quizzing Glass*. The mother of two grown sons, she lives with her professor husband in Texas.

Printed in Great Britain
by Amazon.co.uk, Ltd.,
Marston Gate.